THE STRAIGHT
SHOOTER

A NATE DAINTY MANHUNT!

Visit us at www.boldstrokesbooks.com

Advance Praise for *The Straight Shooter*

"Paul Faraday's *The Straight Shooter* is a light, frothy confection wrapped around a mystery. Nate Dainty is a cute college boy whose latest manhunt is more than just a chase after a cute guy, it's a funny, sexy trek through the world of gay porn."—Neil Plakcy, author of the Mahu mystery series

"*The Straight Shooter: A Nate Dainty Manhunt* is a smart, sexy, fast, and funny plot-twisting page-turner. Paul Faraday takes the reader on a wonderfully madcap West Hollywood sleuthing adventure. Nancy Drew never had this much fun solving a mystery!"—Norah Labiner, author of *German for Travelers* and *Our Sometime Sister*

"Paul Faraday sets up a cool West Hollywood world with fun characters and it's sexy and funny."—Felice Picano, author, Violet Quill member, and winner of the Lambda Literary Foundation Pioneer Award

"*The Straight Shooter* hits dead center, offering a fun, sexy reading experience."—NL Gassert, author of *The Protector*

"A very impressive debut by a major new talent. I look forward to reading more of him."—Greg Herren, author of the Scotty Bradley mystery series

THE STRAIGHT SHOOTER

SHOOTER

A NATE DAINTY MANHUNT!

by

Paul Faraday

A Division of Bold Strokes Books

THE STRAIGHT SHOOTER

ISBN 10: 1-60282-195-X
ISBN 13: 978-1-60282-195-8

This Trade Paperback Original Is Published By
Bold Strokes Books, Inc.
P.O. Box 249
Valley Falls, NY 12185

Printed in the U.S.A.

CREDITS
EDITOR: FELICE PICANO
PRODUCTION DESIGN: STACIA SEAMAN
COVER DESIGN BY SHERI (GRAPHICARTIST2020@HOTMAIL.COM)

Acknowledgments

I want to thank Felice Picano for his unwavering dedication to this manuscript's publication and continued support of new writers. Also, *The Straight Shooter*'s first two readers: my dear friends Andrea Troyer and Carolyn Petrie. Without their encouragement and candor, Nate Dainty would have remained but a glittery sparkle in my eye.

For Eddie, who ended all my manhunts

PART ONE: MYLES LONG

A TOUGH EQUATION

Nate Dainty, you've gone too far!"
Nate Dainty's best friends, cousins Beso Tangelo and Jorge Ramirez, frowned and shook their heads in disapproval at his latest exploit.

"I don't see what's so wrong with registering for Calculus. It certainly beats Judo Kickboxing!" Nate retaliated.

"Well, I hardly think pounding on your calculator is going to burn as many calories as my class, Nate Dainty, so don't be such a critic," Jorge urged. The young, buff Latino crossed his well-chiseled arms and raised an eyebrow at his redheaded pal.

Nate's registering for Calculus was indeed a surprise to the cousins, who had spent three mindless months at the beach, soaking in the sun during their school break. Summer had just ended, and the Los Angeles heat was beginning to wane on this beautiful autumn day.

"Really, Nate, I don't know what you're trying to prove," Beso, Jorge's plump but cute cousin, persisted.

"No more than what you're trying to prove by taking The History of Gay Pop Culture, Beso," Nate replied as he turned his orange BMW convertible into the parking lot of the campus. "Besides, I may just find myself burning more calories than Jorge in his kickboxing class, if things go my way."

"Last time I checked, Nate, there aren't any treadmills in math classes."

"No, but it just happens that a certain someone is registered for Calculus, just like me. And that certain someone definitely has the opportunity to help me burn some calories."

"Oh God, I should have known." Beso held his hands over his eyes melodramatically.

"Don't tell me this is another manhunt of yours, Nate Dainty!"

"It most certainly is," Nate declared as he slung his new book bag over his shoulder and headed to West Hollywood Community College with the cousins. "You wouldn't believe who's taking Calculus with me."

"You're telling us you're taking this sad old class for a man?" Jorge frowned. "Damn, Nate, I thought you learned your lesson last time when you were pursuing *The Barista Who Frothed Too Much* and went broke drinking all those iced mochas."

"And, I, for one," Beso inserted, "had hoped you'd think twice after that painful encounter with *The Hawaiian Who Hung Ten*."

"Not a chance, my friends. This time is different. The man of my summertime dreams is in that Calculus class, and I'm going to give my all to get to know him. Even if it does mean a few hours of studying each night, I'm giving it a shot." Baffled, the cousins shook their heads. "Just enough to get a shot at *The Straight Shooter* himself."

The cousins gasped in horror and then narrowed their eyes at the young, fair-skinned redhead. "Nate Dainty, you mean you're taking Calculus to pursue Myles Long?"

Myles Long was an up-and-coming porn star whose latest release had caught Nate's eye at the adult bookstore during the course of summer break. *The Straight Shooter*, a tale in which Myles portrays a seemingly straight young ad exec whose basketball gets caught in the net during a heated game, had provided Nate Dainty with hours of entertainment. The tightly lodged ball results in Long's newfound ability to read minds, thereby allowing the hunk to easily explore his pent-up gay fantasies. Although Long's third film, it was the first one in which he was featured in every scene—a sure sign of stardom!

The cousins had chided Nate all summer about his obsession with the film, but that didn't stop Nate from viewing it almost nightly. Myles Long had a laid-back, earthy sexiness, not to mention a whopping huge package, that kept Nate's eyes fixated on the big screen television in his uncle's entertainment room.

Nate smiled at their reaction before turning away from the cousins. "I'd better be on my way. Don't want to be late for the first day. See you after class."

Nate hurried off to the Math & Sciences Building of the campus and dashed into the men's room to check his reflection in the mirror for one final glance before going to class. He flashed his sparkling green eyes in the mirror, smiled to reveal perfectly capped, pearl-like teeth, and sized up his new outfit, consisting of a LASC tank top and cargo shorts. The "mystic cocktail" he'd splurged on the night before (a new innovative way to get a natural-looking tan—ten minutes in the tanning bed and then a spray-on tan for a finish) gave his fair skin a slight glow. He was, for sure, a force to be reckoned with.

And hopefully, Myles Long will agree, Nate thought as he popped a breath mint into his mouth.

"Looks like you're definitely enjoying what you see," a voice from behind said, huskily.

Nate laughed, somewhat embarrassed by his own vanity. "I thought I was alone."

He turned to see a young man with curled, sandy blond hair staring at him.

Nate caught his breath momentarily as he looked the man up and down. His calves poked out of his Capri shorts like lemons. His broad chest glistened with perspiration, soaking the center of his tank top. His sleepy blue eyes sparked with recognition, as though all those times earlier, he had seen Nate watching him, hoping all along they would meet like this.

"Well, you're not alone. But *we* are." The man cornered Nate by the sink and breathed close to his ear. Nate's heart raced; he blinked to make sure he wasn't dreaming.

"You—you're Myles Long," Nate stammered.

"I am." Myles flashed a perfect smile at the redhead. "And who might you be?"

"My name's Nate. I'm—uh—I'm a big fan of your films. I just loved *The Straight Shooter*. It's my favorite!"

"Glad to hear it." Myles focused his attention on Nate's neck, against which he rubbed his lips gently. "But you know, Nate, there's a lot more to life than just movies."

"I know," Nate agreed hastily. "I mean…I've wanted to get to know you as a person! I didn't intend to say all this. I was just going to meet you like a regular guy, but you caught me off guard. In fact, we both have the same class, which we should get going to."

"How about we play hooky?" Myles pulled up Nate's tank top and whistled admiringly. The star squeezed Nate's pectorals before giving his pert nipples an affectionate pinch. "There's never any really important information on the first day. Just all the usual B.S. about how you can't miss class."

"That's exactly it, you *can't* miss the first day." Or *could* he? Nate reached his arms back and pulled his shirt completely off. Halfway to where he wanted to be, Myles proceeded to quickly unbutton Nate's shorts, greedily shoving his hands into their front and back sides.

"Don't worry, I happen to know the professor—well," Myles replied slyly.

Before Nate could protest, Myles pushed him against the wall, his mouth hot, and probing. Nate let Myles' tongue in, feeling rising heat between their cargo shorts. Nate had planned on things building *up* to this—but not quite this quickly. The hot friction of their bodies soaked Nate's chest as he savored each of Myles' hungry kisses. Following the star's cue, Nate hastily undid Myles' shorts. With a gasp, he cupped the star's legendary thick shaft in his hand, helping to remove it from the confines of his briefs. Both of their cocks upright, they rubbed together, savoring the impromptu connection. Looks like I'll burn more calories than Jorge after all, he thought.

The bell's shrill ring signaled the start of class. With a smirk, Myles picked Nate up and pushed him up against the sink, resting his ass against the edge of the basin. Eagerly, he tore at Nate's shorts, pulling them down to his ankles, and then eventually to the ground. "I'd say this beats class any day," he moaned, his hands all over Nate's behind. His backside pushed up against the sink's mirror, Nate pulled Myles' tank top off, his hands resting on the star's solid arms. Closing his eyes, Nate felt Myles' hands exploring, touching him in ways that, a mere fifteen minutes before, he had only dreamt about.

And then it was as if the Random Hook-Up Gods had suddenly frowned upon him! The dreaded sound of the restroom door opening, and the rushed footsteps that followed, broke the spell of their encounter. Nate jumped from the sink, reaching for his shorts, while Myles backed away, fumbling with his visibly erect cock and turning to the wall.

"Oh! Excuse me!" The student's eyes widened at the sight of them, and he dropped his pencil box. Hurriedly, he chased the pencils, which rolled rapidly toward the barely untangled duo. Embarrassed, the student grabbed what he could and rushed into one of the stalls, locking it with a quick snap.

Myles looked at Nate with a conspiratorial smile and licked his lower lip. "Let's say we head outta here and spend some time at my place? My roommate's in class so we'll have the place all to ourselves."

"Sounds good!" Nate agreed. If only all things could work out this well! Eyeing the young porn star as he strode ahead, Nate marveled at the record time in which he'd snagged his latest trick. To think, mere minutes ago, I was going to take Calculus for a whole semester! And now here we are, heading to his place for the real deal, Nate thought as they entered the parking lot.

As Myles searched for his car in the packed lot, a sudden

thought crossed Nate's mind. He'd intended to get to know Myles Long, not just have a single hot encounter. All those visions of candlelit dinners, moonlight walks, nights at the opera! But— What was he thinking? He'd never done any of that stuff, with anyone!

"Something wrong?" Myles asked, squeezing Nate's hand as his eyes continued to scan the parking lot.

"No. I was just hoping we could get to know each other. I mean, you're hot and everything! Don't get me wrong. But...I don't know...there's just something different about you. All those times I watched you on film, it was about more than just the sex."

There, he'd said it!

"Really?" Myles eyes lit up.

Was Nate destroying the mood? "I bet you hear that all the time. I just...well, I was taking the class to hope to get to know you better. Not just get into your pants!"

"So, you *don't* want to do it?" Myles asked, his face clouded with disappointment.

"No! I mean, yes! I do." Damn, he was making this difficult. "I guess I wanted both. That sounds silly, I know."

"Not really," Myles answered gently. "Look, Nate, why don't we just head to my place and see what happens." His blue eyes sparkled with anticipation as he took Nate's arm and led him toward his car. Just as he disarmed the alarm to the C500, a loud screech sounded from behind them.

"Nate, watch out!" Myles warned, pushing Nate down between the cars.

As he did, a late-model blue van swerved into the side of his Mercedes.

"What the hell?" Myles swore as a burly, leather-clad man wearing an eye-mask jumped out of the driver's side. From the passenger side, another leather-clad man with a similar eye-mask leapt toward Myles, grabbing his Calculus textbook out of his hands and clubbing him over the head with it. Myles slumped into the second man's arms. Nate noticed a large cobra tattoo on the assailant's right shoulder.

Adjusting his cargo shorts from earlier entanglements, Nate ran forward to save his newfound pal as the two men carried Myles Long and threw him in the back of the van.

"Stop immediately! I'm calling the police," Nate yelled, reaching for his cell phone.

The leather-clad driver came at him growling, and clenching his fists. "Come here, boy! Gimme that phone!" He rushed Nate and attempted to grab the phone. Nate struggled, but he was no match. Meanwhile, the abductor began dragging Nate toward the van!

"This'll teach you to get all sassy with me, boy!" the kidnapper growled as Nate struggled to escape.

Out of the corner of his eye, Nate saw Jorge and Beso nearing the parking lot. Class was over!

"Jorge! Beso! Help!" The two rushed toward Nate and the leather man. "You better watch out! My friend knows judo!" Nate warned, omitting the kickboxing part.

"Oh fuck it!" The thug pushed Nate to the ground in frustration. Nate could make out the abductor's dark, penetrating eyes behind his eye-mask. With a loud bellow, the man angrily slammed his fist on the trunk of Long's Mercedes. Backing off, eyes fixed on Nate, he turned and ran back to the driver side of the van, got in, and the van tore out of the parking lot, onto Robertson Boulevard.

"*Dios mío*, Nate Dainty! What's going on here?" Jorge reached Nate, with Beso's assistance helping him up off the concrete.

"Why weren't you in class?" Beso challenged.

Nate brushed himself off and repositioned his book bag over his shoulder. "We've gotta track down that van! Those brutes kidnapped Myles Long and left me with a nasty case of blue balls!"

BOYNAPPED!

S o I don't get it," Beso said. "Why weren't you in class in the first place?"

"Beso! Catch up, they hooked up in the restroom."

"How vile!" Beso shuddered. "When we file the police report, let's omit that part. I don't want to see my good pal behind bars!"

"We're not going to the police station." Nate hung a left onto Melrose Avenue. The fall breeze picked up and lightly tousled his red hair, giving him that "freshly fucked" look. If only it were *true*, Nate thought ruefully as he examined himself in the rearview mirror.

"We have to report this!" Beso turned to Jorge for support.

"Not until I'm sure that this was truly an abduction. I don't want to report something to the police that may have merely been some kinky exploit!"

"Nate." Jorge sighed exasperatedly. "You don't really think the kidnapping was role-playing, do you?"

"Well, one can never be too sure. I mean, this *is* West Hollywood, I *was* dealing with a hot porn star, and those leather studs were a bit *made-up* to be real thugs. How embarrassing would it be if I reported this, only to find out it was all a sex game?"

"How can you find out for sure?" Beso challenged.

"That is already figured out, my dear Beso." Nate smirked as they headed toward La Brea Avenue.

Nate had read plenty about Myles Long during his summer break and had completed some lengthy Internet research to learn a few important truths about the star. One such important truth was Myles' interest in mathematics and, most recently, in Calculus. Another was Myles' real name: Bobby Roman. On a few occasions, Nate had been guilty of driving by Bobby Roman's residence, a modest fifties walk-up in the Miracle Mile area of L.A. that he shared with a roommate, one Phil Templeton.

Since Nate had accidentally found himself in front of the flat on those occasions, it was hardly a challenge to locate now, was it?

"Hopefully Phil Templeton will be home so that we can get to the bottom of this mess!"

The trio was pleased to find young Phil Templeton in. He was a bookish guy in his mid-twenties, and was checking his mail as they approached the residence. Nate immediately introduced himself to the Nerdster, who'd been balancing his laptop bag on his knee as he opened the mailbox.

"Hello, Mr. Templeton, my name is Nate Dainty and these are my friends Jorge Ramirez and Beso Tangelo. We're wondering if we could have a moment of your time?"

Phil raised an eyebrow from behind thick frames and eyed the three, stopping at Jorge. He began to stammer nervously at the sight of Beso's hunky cousin. "I am supposed to complete a website for a friend of mine. But I guess that could...wait," he said, with a soft note of excitement in his voice.

Nate laughed and patted Phil on the shoulder. "I think you have the wrong idea! We just wanted to ask you a few questions about your roommate, Bobby Roman."

Phil's eager expression changed to one of disappointment. "Also known as Myles Long. Sure! It figures. Look, I'm not his fan club president, and we're just roommates. So if you don't mind, I have work to do."

Nate followed Phil into the doorway. "We're not here for that. I mean, yes, we are fans of Myles Long. But something happened to him that we thought you should know about."

Phil stood at the doorway, leaning, vulnerable. "Don't tell me…the rent's due in five days. I don't have the money to—"

Jorge interrupted the geeky student. "Your roommate is fine. Well, at least we think he is! We just need to ask a few questions to make sure we're not overreacting."

The young student/web designer allowed them into the modest flat, slicking down his black hair nervously when Jorge passed by. Nate took in every detail of the living room: the crown molding, stripped birch floors, and fresh coat of off-white paint. A photo of Myles Long sat on the end table, next to a large, overstuffed, denim slip-covered sofa. Clearly, Nate reasoned, residual checks from the outrageous success of *The Straight Shooter* had not yet arrived!

Nate related the events that had taken place earlier that morning.

Upon hearing the story, Phil stood up from the sofa and removed his glasses, revealing thoughtful brown eyes.

"That doesn't sound like Bobby! He wouldn't do anything like that. It's not like him to get into rough stuff. I've known him since high school, and the only reason he even got into porn in the first place was to pay his way through school."

"That's what they all say," Beso quipped.

Nate jabbed Beso in the side. "I can see that. He does seem like a very honest, hardworking guy. That's what makes him so special…"

"Look, we've taken enough of your time." Jorge pulled Nate toward the doorway. "I think the best thing for us to do now is report this to the police and go home."

"I don't know if that would be a wise idea just yet," Phil interrupted, a look of panic crossing his face before he regained control. "What I mean is…I don't think Bobby would want the media to get hold of this…information. He's very private. The last thing he wants is this little side business interfering with him getting into medical school."

"He wants to be a doctor?" Nate questioned excitedly.

"Nate, he would be perfect," Beso squealed.

"If we don't call the police, then what *would* you recommend?" Nate asked.

"Why don't we keep in touch over the next forty-eight hours to see if anything turns up. Let's exchange numbers and let each other know if we come across any information or, better yet, if we see Bobby. If nothing turns up, then let's contact the police."

The trio agreed, as it was too early to file a missing persons report anyway. Nate and Phil exchanged numbers.

"Perhaps," Phil cautiously eyed Jorge from behind his thick frames, "I could have *your* number, too. In case I can't get hold of Nate."

"Ooh," Jorge said, "I think you'll be able to get a hold of my good *amigo* Nate here just fine!"

Heading back to the car, Nate sighed loudly. "Then it's true! Myles Long really was boynapped! Now what?"

"I think we need to...eat lunch!" Beso opined. "I'm starving!"

"And I have to study," Jorge added, "I have a quiz tomorrow in Judo Kickboxing on strikes and thrusts!"

Nate agreed to drop the two off at a nearby coffee shop for lunch and a study break while he proceeded home to freshen up.

Since the tragic death of Nate's parents when he was two years old, the young redhead had lived with his gay uncle, prestigious entertainment lawyer Carter Dainty. Despite Carter frequently attending movie premieres, contract disputes, and White Parties, the distinguished lawyer still made time to watch after his lively nephew. This week, however, Carter was in Chicago, negotiating a new contract for a high-profile talk-show host client. This left Nate in the hands of Carter Dainty's reliable, if rapidly aging, houseboy, Hans.

"Oh, there you are, Nathan!" Hans said with delight, grabbing him tightly. "I just finished making a delicious lunch for you, and was hoping you'd be home." Hans proudly gestured toward the dining room where a feast of roast beef, steamed broccoli, and tossed salad awaited.

"Hans, this is incredible," Nate said in amazement, "and so very Atkins Diet–friendly!"

"As you know, your sweet Hans is not getting any younger and sadly," Hans said as he inhaled tightly and sucked in his middle before exhaling heavily, "not getting any thinner! As a result, everyone in the house is on a diet! You should invite that friend of yours, Beso, to join us," he hinted with a wink. The weathered houseboy pulled at his tight madras print pants before settling into the dining room chair. "Now tell me! How was your first day at school? I want to know everything!"

Nate quickly informed Hans of every detail, including his encounter with Myles Long.

"How intriguing! You have finally met a man who may just be able to keep you enthralled longer than forty-eight hours! Oh, Nathan, how I recall those days! If I were you, I would enjoy them all that I could."

"There's a catch, Hans." Nate told Hans in detail about the mysterious kidnapping. The houseboy leaned back in his chair with a look of dismay and shock before rising from the table and clearing the plates, clicking his tongue and shaking his head at the revelation.

"Don't even begin to tell me this has turned into yet *another* one of your manhunts!" Hans loaded the dishwasher and then popped an appetite suppression pill. "Why must you always make love into such a challenge?" he asked.

"I don't know, Hans. But I *have* to find him. Right now, my only clue is that the two leather men looked too made-up to be real thugs."

"They were from Silverlake, no doubt! Just be careful, Nathan! Your uncle would never forgive me if something happened to you while he was on a business trip!"

Their conversation was interrupted by the phone ringing. Hans promptly answered and, after a brief exchange, handed the phone to Nate, rolling his eyes. "It's George! For you!"

Hans quickly exited the kitchen, retiring to the den for a fatiguing afternoon of talk shows and courtroom dramas.

"Nate, have you found anything out?" Jorge queried.

"I just finished lunch."

"*Perfecto,*" Jorge responded, "Beso and I are at The Tavern having cocktails and it's Stripper Happy Hour! You need to get here, pronto! Some of the strippers are porn stars. I think I recognize one from *The Straight Shooter*!"

A NOT-SO-GLORIOUS EXCHANGE

Nate entered the bar, surprised by the large late-afternoon crowd that had already gathered for the happy hour festivities. The Tavern, on Santa Monica Boulevard, had become a favorite of Nate and his pals over the summer when it gained a liquor license and went from being a modest coffee shop to an over-the-top meat market that left the denizens of West Hollywood satiated by its combination of coffee, pastries, liquor, and hot summer flings. Even though a slight early autumn chill tinged the air, this night looked no different. The bar was packed with a well-coifed and well-manicured crowd of all ages, gathering and chatting amidst strippers gyrating atop the bar. Careful not to trip on anyone's martini, the dancers tiptoed and wiggled their way down the bar counter, collecting dollar bills, and toying tugs from many of their new admirers.

Nate spotted his friends across the bar, already into their second cocktail by the time he joined them. The cousins jumped up and gave Nate big hugs, Beso squealing, even though it had only been a few hours since they'd parted.

"This is some study break you're having!" Nate chided, entertained by the liveliness of his pals. "Is it true? Is one of the strippers really from *The Straight Shooter*?"

"I can't be certain," Jorge said. "I haven't seen it a million trillion times like you have, Nate Dainty, but the more I drink, the more he looks like he should be the star of something!"

PAUL FARADAY

"Jorge wants him to be the star of his *bedroom*!" Beso laughed, obviously loosened up by his white wine spritzer. "He just went back to freshen up for his next performance. But he should be back soon!"

Jorge repositioned himself on the bar stool, merely glancing at the present dancer, a tan, hunky bleach blond with a neon-pink g-string. "He can take his time. I'm open to exploring options! Anyway, the other dancer looks like the one who's in the scene with Myles Long."

"Which one?" Nate was getting impatient with Jorge's vodka-induced ambiguity.

"The second scene, the one after his basketball becomes stuck in the net."

"The one where Myles goes gay and begins to hear everyone's thoughts," Beso added, flagging the bartender for another round.

Jorge nodded. "Yes. He's the guy in the elevator that's been wanting to screw Myles for years!"

Nate knew the scene well, perhaps too well. His DVD was worn out and it now skipped in this particular scene as a result of his heavy viewing.

In the midst of a heated game with a challenging opponent, Myles Long finds his basketball stuck in the net and, despite numerous attempts, cannot dislodge it. On his way to work, he begins to hear voices, varied in tone and interest, as he passes pedestrians on the street. "What a strange day," Myles says to himself as he nears the office, ready for a regular day's work.

It's in the next scene, when Myles enters the elevator of his office building, that things begin to click, and the significance of the ball getting stuck in the net is revealed to be more than originally thought.

Despite the conversation around him, Nate couldn't help but fall back into the scene he had viewed so many times that summer.

Myles Long, in a business suit, boarding the elevator with

another man, in a similar suit, but with a thick mustache and dark, smoldering, somewhat rough-around-the-edges good looks. He follows Myles in and both head to the top floor.

However, when the door closes, time seems to freeze—there's a close-up of the dark and handsome guy as his thoughts are revealed to Myles. "I've been riding in the elevator with this guy for years…what I'd give to have the chance to screw him!" The thought echoes as Myles arches an eyebrow, smirks slightly, and then begins to make out with the businessman.

As the elevator climbs, more and more clothing is removed, until both are naked, savoring each kiss, sweating heavily during the encounter. The once conservative young ad exec, now ensconced inside the thoughts of his once-secret admirer, lets himself go, sliding to the bottom of the elevator and taking Buck Steers' large shaft into his mouth. Their suits are now piled on the elevator floor. Myles slides back up to face the exec. And slowly turns him around, for the fucking of a lifetime!

After both hunks shoot their plentiful wads on the elevator carpet and dress, they conveniently depart onto the twelfth floor, where both go their separate ways.

And now, after a quick break, the costar of that scene, Buck Steers, had returned and was off to the side of the bar, his brown eyes focused directly at Nate's best friend, Jorge.

Jumping from a side door close to the bar and catapulting himself atop the counter, to the cheers and delight of the crowd, Buck commanded attention as he began dancing. Although Buck Steers was not necessarily his type, Nate had to admit that he was pretty hot. All six feet of him glistened, emitting a raw masculinity that the small screen didn't do justice to. Nate's eyes made their way along Buck's solid and well-chiseled body, stopping suddenly at the sight of a large cobra tattoo on his right shoulder. Running his hand over tousled dark hair, Buck kept his chestnut eyes on Jorge as he bent his legs down and lowered his cash-stuffed leather g-string before him.

"Don't go breaking the bank, Jorgito," Beso said as he sipped his spritzer.

"I was hoping for a phone number," Buck said softly before turning to reveal two firm, slightly hairy, melon-shaped buttocks, parted only by a thin strap of black leather. Not one to waste time, Jorge quickly scribbled his number before placing it between the leather and Buck Steers' glistening olive skin.

"That's all my contact info," Jorge revealed, attempting to cover a slight stammer. "Home phone, cell phone, and e-mail... Call me."

"Will do, stud," Buck winked with a smile before hopping off the bar top and exiting into the changing room. A moment of possible recognition went through Nate's mind. But as he turned to do a second take, the star was gone.

"That was amazing!" Nate exclaimed, wrapping his arm around Jorge's shoulder. "What incredible luck!"

"I'll say," Beso said. "Looks like you'll have quite a time with him. Just be sure to keep it all under wraps—if you know what I mean? After all, he *is* a porn star."

"And to think he may help us find out what happened to Myles Long," Nate reminded them. "I hate to say it, Jorge, but I think Buck Steers may be just the lead we need on tracking him down."

"Why on earth would you think that?" Jorge snapped. "They starred in one scene together, Nate. It's not like they were best friends. Besides, for once, it would be nice if I could enjoy the company of another *hombre* without you tying it in to one of your manhunts!"

"That's just it, Jorge," Nate pursued. "As Buck Steers was leaving, I recognized the tattoo on his left shoulder. The cobra?"

"I saw it, too. What does that have to do with anything?" Jorge was clearly upset by Nate's own pursuit.

"I know it sounds crazy, Jorge, but I think one of Myles Long's abductors had that *same tattoo*! He was the one I didn't get to catch a very good glimpse of, the one on the passenger side.

He was wearing a mask, and a leather biker cap, which made it hard to recognize him for certain. But the tattoo is exactly the same!"

"Absolute nonsense, *cabron*!" Jorge rebutted. "There must be thousands of bears, cubs, and leather daddies in this city with cobra tattoos. And I'm sure if someone of Buck Steers' stature has one, then there must be plenty of wannabes sporting the same tat."

Before Nate could say anything else, the dance music stopped and the lights dimmed more, drawing a hush amongst the now-intoxicated crowd. "Ladies and gentlemen and not-so-gentle-men, The Tavern is proud to announce for tonight only a special fashion extravaganza," the announcer, a heavyset black drag queen, proclaimed as she sipped from her signature oversized martini glass. "Here, for a sneak preview of her winter line, fashion designer, real estate magnate, socialite, and hmmm, let's see, what else does she do?...oh yes, and gay porn production mogul, Miss Anitra Tucci!"

Amidst the crowd's applause, Nate Dainty dug his fingers into Jorge's shoulder and jumped up and down with excitement, just as the well-known producer climbed atop the flimsily constructed stage. In a robin's-egg blue power suit, micro-mini, and chocolate-colored stilettos, Anitra Tucci looked fabulous. Smiling broadly, she grabbed the microphone, exchanged air kisses with the drag queen, and lightly brushed her frosted hair out of her heavily made-up face before addressing the crowd.

"Thank you, all! And thank you, Ana Bender, for those kind words. Just hearing about all of those titles makes it hard for even *me* to keep track of what *I've* been up to these days." She paused momentarily for some light tittering among the audience. "And while I'm sure many of you are keenly aware of what I've been doing in terms of video entertainment, I know that at least some have been keeping track of what will be my biggest project to date."

Turning, the diva took a manicured claw and pulled a sheet

from the wall, revealing a marquee-sized sign in bold pink letters:

TANK TOPS BY TUCCI

Amidst the hushed conversations that ensued, Anitra smiled broadly and addressed the intrigued crowd. "For those of you that like to keep up on all the latest trends in West Hollywood, I'm sure you're aware of the very limited release of my signature tank tops this past summer. I even saw a young lad over there!— wearing one. Excuse me, you with the blond crew cut and a smile that lasts for days, please stand."

The young hunk hesitantly stood, and the spotlight turned to his chest, covered tightly by an army green tank top that read in bold yellow print, *I Reserve the Right to Inspect All Packages*.

The crowd laughed loudly in recognition of the shirt, which had been worn all around L.A., and had even been seen worldwide at the occasional circuit party.

"And I'm here to tell you all," Anitra went on, "that you truly ain't seen nothin' yet! This is just the beginning of what is sure to be the hottest trend not only here in WeHo, but quite possibly the entire world. Introducing, here tonight, *exclusively* at The Tavern, the first official showing of Tank Tops by Tucci International. Ladies and gents, our Winter Line!"

Applause echoed throughout the room, as a high-energy dance tune got louder along with the swirling lights on stage. A young, thin guy with tattoos and a short, dark Mohawk arrived onstage, clad in bikini briefs and a tight-fitting tank top proclaiming *Parties of Eight of More Will Be Charged an 18% Gratuity*. Scowling and grabbing himself, he eyed the audience as if it was prey, preening as he went from the stage to the bar top, modeling Anitra Tucci's latest creation.

"Now, boys, I know it does get cold out *even here* in the winter time, and for some of you, a tank top may not be the most *practical* garment to wear during inclement weather," Anitra admitted from one side of the stage. "But I have a solution that will allow you to show off those well-defined biceps, triceps, and pecs you've all worked so hard on."

She sighed and batted her eyes coquettishly. "It's just a shame none of you pitch for my team. What's a girl to do?" The crowd again laughed at the entrepreneuress as she pouted. "We all know that during the cold, nothing's more attractive than an erect nipple or two, but the flu or cold that might ensue soon after too much exposure is anything but! So for that, my team of designers has put together the perfect accessory for my winter tank tops: a nice warm scarf! Felipe, would you demonstrate?" From the side of the stage, the Mohawked model caught a thick knit scarf and proceeded to drape the striped, fuzzy number around his neck. In unanimous approval, the crowd cheered and clapped.

"This way, we can all keep warm while still displaying our wares. Isn't that right, Felipe?"

"I *love* it," Jorge exclaimed. "I've been trying to figure out how to show off the merchandise without getting the *pinche gripa*. This really solves all my troubles!"

"I'm sure Buck Steers wouldn't object to you wearing one of those on your first date," Beso said, frowning slightly. "Although I'm actually looking forward to some nice warm sweaters and scarves and jackets—anything to cover up this extra fifteen pounds." He crossed his arms over the offending belly.

"Let's not forget," Nate reminded the cousins, "Anitra Tucci is also the producer of *The Straight Shooter*."

"And, gathering from her calm and controlled stage presence, she probably has no idea that her star Myles Long has been abducted." Beso turned to Nate. "Now's your chance to let her know!"

It didn't take much encouraging. The moment the show ended and The Tavern's patrons returned to their normal conversation and incessant cruising, Nate Dainty joined the small group of admirers that went to speak to Tucci. One by one, they praised her designs, her real estate acquisitions, and, most often, her inimitable skill for capturing hot man-sex on film.

"All in a day's work," Tucci purred as she made her way through the crowd. "Be sure to check out my website for a pre-sale of my latest line."

Just as she was about to exit behind the stage, Nate made an attempt to stop the multitalented maven.

"Excuse me, Ms. Tucci," Nate called, but Anitra continued her charge backstage, whipping off her pale blue blazer as she entered the changing room.

"The lighting was all wrong!" she wailed at a nervous young man who stood with a clipboard, slapping him across the head and knocking his telephone headset to the ground. "Next time, why don't you just do the fashion show at a goddamn Kmart? I'll be the next Jaclyn Fucking Smith!"

"Sorry, Ms. Tucci," he apologized, his eyes tearing up.

"We're having this show to sell tank tops, Elvin! Have you ever, in your small, uninteresting little life, had to sell five hundred thousand tank tops?"

The man shook, his lip quivering in terror.

"Well, *have you?*" she challenged, to which he shook his head. "I didn't think so. Now, go out there and get some orders, or you're as good as fired!" The man picked up his headset and exited quickly, taking note of Nate Dainty at the entrance.

"I wouldn't go in there if I were you," he advised before running right to the bar. From outside the changing room, Nate heard Tucci wail once again. "And what about the rest of you? *Go out there and sell tank tops!*" Three scantily clad models ran out of the changing room, their hands full of freshly folded tank tops.

"Somebody needs a saucer of milk!" Felipe, the Mohawked model, declared upon leaving. Ignoring the obvious warnings, Nate made his way into the room.

"Excuse me! Ms. Tucci?" he called again.

"What?" she snapped, coming face-to-face with the redhead. Her green eyes glowed warmly as her initial sneer turned into a sudden smile. "Ah, if only we'd met earlier. You would have been perfect for *Code Red*, my new redhead fetish film. What can I do for you?"

"I need to talk to you about Myles Long—he's missing. And I'm worried that if we don't find him soon, it may be too late!" Nate quickly filled the porn producer in on what had occurred earlier.

Anitra shook her head in disbelief, gazing at her reflection in the changing room mirror. "That explains why Myles didn't show up for my tank top fashion show this evening. I've been so flustered with this entire…production, I'd forgotten all about his absence. This is indeed a puzzle."

"Do you think," Nate continued carefully, "that Myles would be involved with these guys as some sort of role-playing scene?"

Tucci threw her head back with a controlled laugh, her heavily sprayed coif making a scratching sound against her collar. "My dear Myles Long in a *role-playing* scenario? Never! That angel would never participate in such an ill-reputed… No! I have a feeling this is linked directly to Chapped Hide!"

"Chapped Hide?"

"Oh," Tucci said dismissively, "It's a ramshackle old production company in the Valley. For whatever reason, they've been trying to make a comeback, and to do so, they've been stealing all my stars! I know they were making some pretty outrageous offers to Myles, but he wasn't interested." Her face turned grave with concern. "Perhaps they wouldn't take no for an answer."

"That might explain why those leather clad thugs looked so well-groomed," Nate reasoned, eyeing the woman. Despite her earlier fury, Tucci had regained control of her mercurial temper and softened into the classy lady the press always touted her to be.

"The media would have a heyday with this news," Tucci realized, pacing the changing room with her arms folded.

"I can only imagine," Nate said, "the panic that might erupt among your other stars."

"Yes," Tucci noted, "and for that reason I'm going to have to ask you to do me a favor. Please don't mention this to the police or anyone else until I decide to."

"But, Ms. Tucci, are you sure we *have* time to *spare*?"

"My *friends*, Nate Dainty, all call me Anitra, and I suggest you do the same," she purred. "Besides, with us working together, I'm sure we can do more than any mere police department."

She extended a hand to Nate Dainty and looked at him intently. "Now do we, or do we not, have a deal?"

Seduced by her commanding style, Nate shook her hand firmly in agreement. "Deal!"

❖

Beso wandered into The Tavern restroom and washed his hands, catching a quick glimpse of his reflection in the mirror. In the dim light, his brown skin glowed, complementing his hazel eyes. Brushing his overgrown shag cut with one hand, he turned to one side and examined his profile. If I start a diet now, he thought, I should be able to squeeze into one of those sassy tank tops by the spring.

Just as he was about to make his way back to the bar, a puff of moist air hit him in the neck, releasing a sweet, floral aroma. Clutching his neck in horror and turning behind him, he came face-to-face with the restroom attendant. "What are you doing?" Beso demanded, coughing at the over-sweet odor.

"Complimentary sample of Forbidden Passion, just for you." The attendant, an elderly man, gazed at him, the cologne bottle still in tow.

"I don't *want* a complimentary sample," Beso cried. "I just came here to freshen up."

"Now you're fresh as a daisy," the man replied primly, setting the bottle down and drying up the water spots along the sinks.

"Now I smell like a rotting cantaloupe!" Beso grabbed a folded washcloth from the attendant's basket.

"Washcloths," the man said without looking up from his cleaning, "are five dollars."

"Five dollars!" Beso exclaimed. "I don't think so!" Running hot water over the towel, Beso walked into the restroom stall and removed his shirt, hanging it carefully over the hook. He wiped the damp cloth liberally over his neck and chest, hoping to remove as much of the offensive scent as possible. It seems like everyone's found a hot guy to chase after except for me, he thought, sighing.

Just at that moment, he noticed someone step into the stall next to him, running his fingers along a carved-out hole in the divider.

Good gravy, Beso thought, this restroom stall has a glory hole! That's so...trashy! But I'm sure somehow they must be a part of Gay Pop Culture History! Just for research purposes, it would be interesting to see exactly who or what is on the other side.

Without another moment's hesitation, a large thick shaft slipped through the newly discovered hole. Beso gasped with excitement; the effect of the white wine spritzers had begun to numb his usually more pristine sensibility. His mouth parted slightly as he admired the throbbing veins of the newly discovered pleasure tool. "My gosh," he murmured to himself, "it'd be a shame to pass up this hands-on opportunity to explore Gay Pop Culture!" After covering the floor of the restroom with a paper toilet seat cover, Beso got down on his knees and inspected the large head admiringly. Closing his eyes in anticipation, he opened his mouth and wrapped his lips around it. The thick cock throbbed in appreciation as Beso took it in, quickly plunging to the back of his throat. Surprised by the man's size, Beso let it fall out and leaned back, gasping for air, watching the shaft before him continue to harden. Wanting more, Beso leaned forward, allowing the man back into his mouth. From the other side of the wall, he could hear the soft moans of his recipient. The shaft rubbed against Beso's lips and lightly slapped his face before shoving back into his mouth, forcing his jaw wider, and making him take the cock down deeper than he thought was possible. Beso could feel himself loosening up, the sensation of the cock becoming hotter, and tension building to what he knew was sure to be an explosive moment.

"Yeah, take it," the man moaned, his pleasurable words muffled by the intervening stall. With a sense of awe and even some disbelief, Beso continued to suck, his jaw aching, as the man continued to stab with faster, shorter thrusts. There was no question: he was near his climax. Eagerly, Beso continued, sucking him hungrily. Suddenly, just as the man's cock began to throb in that wonderfully familiar way, he felt the penis slide back into the other stall, and a hand, now in the shaft's place, grab him by the side of the mouth.

Oh My God, Beso thought, the one time I decide to suck cock at a glory hole and look what happens! Just as he was about to scream, he felt a large, crumpled stale object cram into this mouth. Then he heard the cruiser in the other stall flush and run away.

Coughing, his eyes watering, Beso got up and pulled the object from his mouth.

It was a piece of crumpled yellow legal paper with writing in dark blue ink. Carefully unraveling the paper, Beso gasped in horror as he realized the note was meant for him: *Back Off, Fat Fuck! And Tell Your Gal Pal, Nate Dainty, to Mind His Biz!*

UP IN FLAMES!

A s the show wound to a close, the strippers said farewell to their admirers and began to head home, or headed off to negotiate better rates elsewhere. Nate barely noticed when the lights dimmed and the music shifted into a different, slower-paced track. His thoughts wandered back to his earlier encounter with Myles Long. He had been so close to sleeping with the man of his summer dreams, and those thugs had ruined his chances! He was relieved at the coincidence of meeting Anitra Tucci for the first time, but would she really help him in catching the men who'd kidnapped Myles? A tap on the shoulder from Jorge snapped him back into reality.

"I would love to stay with you boys for another round." Jorge's arms were full of recently purchased tank tops. "But I have a hot date with a certain Buck Steers I just can't pass up."

"I can't say I blame you," Nate encouraged, then informed his good friend of his conversation with Tucci. "Fill me in on all the details, and don't forget to find out as much as you can about—"

"About Myles Long," Jorge finished, sighing heavily. "I'll do what I can, but first I'm going to take Buck Steers to Los Ojos and have my way with him." And with that, the buff young friend took off into the darkness. Glancing back at the bar, Nate saw Beso running toward him, panicked. He approached breathing heavily, leaning against the table exhausted. Nate noticed marks on his khakis as well as an overall wrinkled appearance that normally would have made Beso shudder.

"Nate," Beso demanded, "where's Jorge?"

"Just missed him! Beso, what's wrong? My God, where's my Tide Stick when I need it? You're a wreck!"

"Look." Beso unfolded the message he'd received. "We're in serious danger, Nate! We need to stop this whole search and go back to a happier, simpler time—immediately!"

Nate examined the message carefully before slipping the paper into his shirt pocket. "Who could have written this? Beso, where did you find this note? And, while we're on the subject, why does it have your Wild Cherry ChapStick all over it?"

"I'll explain all that once we get home," his plump sidekick insisted as he looked around the bar. "Where's Jorge? He's coming, too, no?"

"You're too late. Jorge just left with Buck Steers."

"We *can't* leave the two of them alone!"

"Beso—"

"I can't explain it, Nate, but something tells me Jorge is headed for trouble! We all are, if we don't get ourselves out of this mess."

"Mess? Beso! Calm down. We haven't done anything, aside from visiting Phil Templeton and asking Anitra Tucci a question or two." Resting a calming hand on his pal's shoulder, Nate convinced Beso to sit and have a glass of water. Beso thirstily gulped the water, struggling to catch his breath.

"Beso, where did you get this note?"

Pausing momentarily, Beso let out a slow breath. "Oh, Nate. It was awful! I was in the restroom when I was attacked from behind. I tried to scream, but the person who grabbed me shoved this note in my mouth!"

"This doesn't make sense. Not many people know we're searching for Myles. It could have been Phil Templeton, or one of those thugs from the campus parking lot figured out who I was. Or it could have even been Anitra Tucci!"

"Oh no, I *doubt that*," Beso protested. "I don't think Anitra has that much...er...strength. I was handled very roughly, Nate. Look, I'd love to tell you more, but I'm also concerned that the attacker might have been Buck Steers himself!"

"Beso! What are you *not* telling me?"

Beso shrugged his shoulders and leaned in, his tone hushed. "Nate Dainty, sometimes you're just too perceptive for my own good. The real reason I think it could be Buck Steers, the real reason I know why it *wasn't* Anitra Tucci, is because I did see a certain part of my attacker, but only for a moment."

Nate looked at his chum before his eyes widened with discovery. "You mean to say you saw your attacker's penis? Beso Tangelo, were you in the Stall Three's glory hole?"

"It was research for my Gay Pop Culture class! What's a girl to do? It was the hottest, thickest cock I've ever seen!"

"Which means it could have belonged to a porn star, model, or strip dancer, of which there are more than one in the bar this evening. But if you think it's Buck Steers, perhaps we can go back to my place and watch *The Straight Shooter*, and check it out."

"Or we could go find my cousin, split them apart, and tear that monster's pants off!" Beso snapped. He was, after all, a victim of glory hole rejection.

"Jorge did mention that he was taking Buck out for a romantic night at Los Ojos..."

"Then what are we waiting for?" Beso urged. *"Vámonos!"*

❖

With Buck Steers' car close behind, Jorge maneuvered his Mini Cooper into the small paved area in front of his trailer home. Jorge had lived for years in Los Ojos, a charming, gay-friendly trailer park just over the Hollywood Hills, in Valley Village. On occasion, Beso had also stayed there with his cousin, particularly on dollar-drink nights at the Adobe, their favorite gay bar in the Valley. Jorge's two-bedroom trailer was by far the best-looking one on its block, outfitted with Jorge's own personal touches of faux stone exterior, stamped concrete entrance, and granite counter tops.

Walking along the front entrance, Jorge fussed with a bird of paradise bloom that had slumped over the sidewalk as the headlights of Buck's car approached and clicked off as he parked beside the Mini Cooper.

In the late evening, the trailer park was silent. Watching Buck get out of the car, his well-built frame approaching the sidewalk, Jorge had to pinch himself to make sure he wasn't dreaming!

"Welcome to *mi casa*." Jorge grabbed Buck's hand, leading him in the trailer.

"Nice place," Buck looked around as he flipped a backpack over his shoulder, "and worth the drive!" He moved in and kissed Jorge, wrapping his arms around him as they made their way into the house.

"Damn," Jorge moaned. "You've got me so worked up." He flicked on the dimmed lights of the living room.

Buck stepped back and shook his eyes in disbelief, his mussed hair falling over his face. "To be honest, Jorge, you surprised me tonight." Buck leaned in and gave Jorge another kiss, this one longer than the first, as he proceeded to unbutton Jorge's jeans and do some exploring of his own. The buff Latino could feel his cock growing in response to Buck's skillful hands.

"I know, Buck," Jorge agreed, "I even surprised myself." Smirking sexily in reply, Buck dropped quickly to his knees, teasing the head of Jorge's now fully erect cock through the material. Leaning back, Jorge closed his eyes as he felt Buck's mouth slide over the head of his shaft. "This is exactly what I needed."

"Well, if you're really interested," Buck marveled as he stood back up and touched his backpack nervously, "I guess I'll just use your bathroom to freshen up!"

"Sure. Be my guest." Jorge led Buck to the bathroom. He raced into the bedroom and pulled out a pair of sheer black briefs and matching tank top from the dresser, quickly sliding into them and lighting candles all along the windows and ledges of the room.

Aglow in the soft blaze of the candles, Jorge caught his reflection in the full-length mirror. "Irresistible!" he prided himself, positioning the mirror so that it faced the bed. "There's no way I'm gonna miss a single *segundo* of this night!"

Hearing the bathroom door open, Jorge slipped into the bed, leaning his head back onto his hands as he stretched his legs out.

"Man, my contacts were killing me," Buck said, coming around the corner into the bedroom, his backpack still resting over his shoulder, a thin laptop computer in his right hand.

At the sight of the porn star, Jorge leapt off the bed and examined his Stripper Happy Hour find close-up. Buck Steers leaned against the wall and took in Jorge's sexy appearance as he covered his eyes with a pair of thick corrective glasses, using one hand to slick back his dark hair.

"Why! You're...Phil Templeton?" Jorge gasped, stepping back in disbelief.

❖

Racing along the 101 Freeway, Nate and Beso retraced details of the manhunt so far. Nate filled Beso in as much as possible on his conversation with Anitra Tucci.

"Don't you find it odd she wants you to keep the police out of this?" Beso asked. "I'm thinking we should just call nine-one-one, right now."

"What will that do?" Nate challenged. "How seriously do

you think the police will take this kidnapping? Not to mention the blaze of bad publicity might ruin Myles Long's future career."

"Good point," Beso agreed. "But I'm telling you, Nate Dainty, whoever threatened us tonight was watching us, and I think their glory hole hijinx is only the beginning of the trouble they could cause."

"After what you've told me, I have to agree. But at this point, we're too far in to back out. The fact we're receiving threats only means we're on the right track! Besides, the surroundings have been pleasant to look at while we've been on this little manhunt."

"You mean," Beso said snidely, "the beauty of the One-seventy Lankershim exit?"

"No, silly," Nate corrected him. "All the hot men we keep running into."

Turning a sharp right, Nate steered the car past the post-production studios and car repair shops littering NoHo. They were one of a few cars still on the road this late at night. Realizing that it was 3 a.m., Nate thought back to what the past twenty-four hours had brought. Frightening as it was, he loved the challenge. He thought, if Myles Long finds out I'm the one who saved him, there's no way he'll be able to resist me.

"Ooh, look, Tommy's Burgers," Beso exclaimed with glee. "Stop!"

"But what about your cousin?" Nate wondered.

"I'm sure Jorge will be okay for a *few* more minutes. Besides, he did just take that karate kickboxing class."

They wheeled up to the drive-thru and Nate ordered a side of onion rings while Beso had a chili burger, fries, and a strawberry shake.

"I'm just so hungry, after all those white wine spritzers," the fast-food-fiend explained to his pal.

"Beso, it's not good for you to eat that stuff so late at night," Nate reminded his yo-yo dieter of a friend as he paid the cashier. "I really think you'll end up hating yourself in the morning!"

Before Beso could respond, they heard what sounded like gunfire in the distance.

"Ooooh! Nate, let's get out of here!"

"Do you think that's gunfire?" Nate asked.

"It sure isn't fireworks. Let's get to Los Ojos, and step on it!"

Steering out of the parking lot and back onto the road, they saw the source of the disturbance. A block away, they could see flames shooting high into the sky, with billows of dark smoke covering the moonlit night.

"That's Los Ojos, Nate, we've got to get there, fast!" Beso managed to get out between mouthfuls of his burger going in. "Great, now I'm too nervous to even *eat*!"

As they pulled into the trailer park, they were stopped by a young fireman at the front entrance.

"You can't go in right now. There's a fire spreading throughout the park," the blond firefighter said, his white teeth contrasting nicely with his tough, leathery tan.

Nate stopped and smiled, blushing a bit before reminding himself of why he was here.

"I understand, sir, but we have an emergency on our hands. We're worried my friend, his cousin," Nate gestured at Beso. "Well, we're worried he's in danger. If you could just let us get to Twenty-six Washing Machine Lane…"

"What was the address?" the fireman leaned closer to the car window, his unbuttoned uniform revealing two well-developed pectorals drenched with flame induced perspiration.

Again, Nate paused, the dark, manly scent making the firefighter hard to resist.

"Twenty-six Washing Machine Lane," Nate repeated.

The fireman removed his hat and kneeled closer to the window of Nate's car, his expression solemn.

"I'm really sorry, guys, Twenty-six Washing Machine Lane is where the blaze started. I'm afraid there's nothing left to see. It's burnt to a crisp!"

CHAPPED HIDES

"This...can't...be!" Beso cried hysterically.

Nate turned again to the friendly fireman. "We need to get there. Is there any way you could just move your well-chiseled frame to the side a moment, so we could sneak in?"

The firefighter paused and looked both directions before replying. "Okay. But if anyone asks, I had nothing to do with it."

The two raced toward Washing Machine Lane as the ash from the fire began to coat the car and cause them to cough uncontrollably. Where Jorge's trailer once stood was nothing but his smoldering former belongings. A group of firemen continued to hose down the fire, which had finally begun to surrender to their torrent of water.

As soon as Nate slowed the car, Beso was out, sobbing, as he rushed to the site. "Oh, my *Jorgito*! See, Nate, I told you! I tried to tell you we were in for something terrible. Are you happy now? Jorge's been fried like a *chimichanga*!"

Nate tried to be the voice of reason, but the gravity of the situation was beginning to set in. "I had no idea this would happen, Beso. You have to believe me."

"I absolutely rue the day you started watching that porn with a plot, Nate Dainty. I *rue* the day! Look what all of your masturbatory fantasies have led to!"

From one side of the smoldering ashes, they heard a hoarse cough, rising from an area just left of the playground. Realizing the cough was definitely human, the two rushed over to the figure.

"Oh sweet Jesus, it's Jorge!" Beso cried in excitement.

The two knelt down to help the buff lad sit up. Covered with grime and grit from the blaze, Jorge opened his eyes and smiled with relief upon seeing his two good pals.

"I've never been so happy to see you two in all my life!"

"What on earth happened, Jorge?" Nate asked. "Just over an hour ago, you were saying farewell to us, planning an evening with Buck Steers. And now this?"

"I thought I was going to have an evening of wild fun, too," Jorge replied. "Not quite this wild! Believe me, all I wanted was a hot romp with Buck Steers, but as soon as he got to my *casa*, his entire *caliente persona* changed. We got into my bedroom, and you would—not—believe what happened!"

"Don't tell me," Beso said with a raised hand. "He was into scat!"

"Worse! He put on a pair of thick glasses and began working on a website. Buck Steers, in real life, is none other than—Phil Templeton!"

"What?" Nate asked, offering a wet-nap to his good friend.

"*Sí, hombres*, Phil Templeton! You heard right." Jorge took the wet-nap and wiped soot from his face. "We got to my place and he had this backpack with him. I think, this Buck Steers must be into some crazy-ass shit. But when we got into my bedroom, he removed his contact lenses, whipped out his laptop computer, and channel surfed my TV onto *The Golden Girls*!"

"*The Golden Girls*," Beso squealed. "Maybe *I* should have taken him home instead of you."

Suddenly, beyond anyone's control, all three broke into peals of laughter, relieved that they were all safe together, despite the danger that had come their way.

"But how did the fire start?" Beso inquired. "Don't tell me he was keyboarding so fast it sparked an electrical current!"

"No. You see, boys, I wouldn't give up. I simply had to change the mood. Between the clicking of the keyboard and the laugh track erupting after each of Dorothy's one-liners to Rose Nyland, I knew I was destined for a cold shower if I didn't spice things up quickly! That's when I put on my Shakira CD, lit more candles, and got out some chablis from the fridge." Jorge looked at what remained of his sexy semi-transparent black tank top and undies.

"So, I'm prowling around on the bed, like a sleek black pussycat, smooching on Buck's plump nipples. Oh my God, boys, he had such a hot body, you wouldn't believe what a sweater-vest and khakis can hide from the world. I figured if I could get those big glasses off his face and find a way to rid him of the laptop, I could *still* make a good night of it. But, in the process of this whole seduction, my pillow knocked over one of the candles. Before I knew it, we were surrounded by an uncontrollable blaze! I started coughing, and that's when I think the fire had reached the propane gas tank outside the trailer, because the explosion knocked me all the way over to here!"

At that point, one of the firemen approached the trio. "Excuse me. Is one of you the owner of this…trailer?"

When Jorge identified himself, the fireman solemnly handed him the remains of a black leather thong and a large pair of melted eyeglasses. "I'm afraid that's all we've found of your friend. My apologies on your loss."

Jorge held the thong and glasses for a moment before setting them to the side. "See, boys, even I can't make up this shit. It's *for reals*. Anyway, Nate, what I forgot to tell you is that somewhere in all this madness I found the time to ask about your *precioso* Myles Long."

Nate's ears perked up. "Don't be coy, Jorge Ramirez! Spill the *frijoles*!"

"Well, that's just it. It was kind of strange. When I mentioned Myles' kidnapping again, he just got really nervous. He looked like he wanted to hide behind those thick glasses and forget the whole incident."

"Really?" Nate asked. "Maybe Phil Templeton was involved in the abduction after all."

"For sure he was," Jorge agreed.

"Maybe *he* was the one who wrote that note," Beso continued.

"Note? What are you boys talking about?"

Nate informed Jorge of what had happened at The Tavern.

"Well, that would make sense. I *did* meet up with Buck slash Phil at the parking lot. And he *did* say he had to take care of something real quick. But, Beso, what were you doing in stall three in the first place?"

"It was research for school," Beso wailed. "Can we move on, please?"

"So, anyway," Jorge continued, "when Phil started to avoid the topic, I kept asking questions. Once I pointed out the similarity of his tattoo to one of the abductors, he admitted he was one of the men who had pulled Myles Long into that van. Now granted, at the time he was pretty focused on his website and that *Golden Girls* episode. It was a good one, too. The one where Rose auctions Dorothy off for charity—"

"And Stan has the winning bid," Beso finished. "I *love* that episode!"

"Jorge! Beso!" Nate urged, "Focus! Get to the point!"

"Well, so like I *says*, he wasn't really paying attention, just kind of mumbling stuff. He said that this dude made him an offer he couldn't refuse. He felt bad and all helping with the kidnapping, but he says 'You gotta know better than to cross Mac.'"

"Who is Mac?"

"No idea," Jorge responded. "I was even thinking maybe he

meant 'The Mac,' like maybe Myles was working part-time as a hustler. I mean, he is, after all, a porn star."

"And maybe he was trying to break free," Beso added. "Another story of a down-and-out ho held back by her damn pimp!"

"Beso!" Nate snapped. "How dare you talk that way about Myles Long! But I have a feeling we're onto something, Jorge. Whoever this Mac character is, must be a clue to where Myles is, and what's happened to him."

"Before we go any further," Beso reminded the two, "we need a good night's rest."

"*De acuerdo*," Jorge seconded, "And…I had better call my insurance company. To think of all the *trabajo* I put into my little *casita* and now it's reduced to this!"

Nate put a reassuring hand on his well-muscled shoulder. "We'll help you every step of the way. You know that, Jorge. Beso, I couldn't agree more on needing sleep. We have a big day ahead tomorrow."

"You mean *you* have a big day ahead of you," Beso corrected him. "I don't want anything more to do with this manhunt of yours, Nate Dainty. This plot almost killed my cousin!" He wrapped his arms around his scantily clad relative while attempting to scowl at the loveable redhead.

"Come on, Beso! We might be in danger, but we're not nearly in the same danger Myles Long is. When I spoke to Anitra Tucci, she seemed to think his abduction might be the work of her rival studio, Chapped Hide Productions. According to her, they've been trying to lure Myles to their studio for months."

"Maybe they were tired of playing Mr. Nice Guy," Jorge finished the thought.

The three returned to Nate's house for the evening. There, Hans hastily set up the guest room for Beso and Jorge. With Beso and Jorge asleep, Nate caught up the aging houseboy on the latest details of his manhunt.

"Nathan! This sounds dangerous! If only your uncle was here to talk you out of this."

"Please, Hans, you and I both know my uncle had some very daring adventures of his own when he was my age." The crimson blush that erupted on Hans' heavily tanned face only confirmed that the young spitfire was absolutely correct about his uncle's younger, wild days.

After a good night's sleep, the three friends woke to a breakfast of scrambled eggs, fried bacon, and pineapple pancakes. Once the cooking was complete, Hans joined them momentarily, popping a diet tablet before downing his energy drink.

"Hans, this is absolutely delicious," Beso moaned in delight.

"Thank you, Beso," Hans beamed with pride. "I figure it's better to indulge in the morning than at night. That way you have all day to burn off the calories."

"This is utterly fattening," Jorge snapped. "Tell me, Hans, have you ever even *heard* of egg whites?"

"If you want to make yourself breakfast, George, then go home!" Hans retorted. "I hear there's a burnt-up old trailer with *your* name on it!"

"Oh really?" Jorge stood up to the challenge.

"Now, boys," Nate said, "let's stay focused on what we're all here for. We don't have time for petty arguments." Obligingly, the three thanked Hans for the delicious breakfast and set off for the porn studios of far Van Nuys.

"Do you need directions on how to get there?" Hans asked.

"Why? Do you go there often?" Jorge replied, his eyes squinting in fury. Hans shoved the directions to Chapped Hide he had printed from MapQuest earlier that morning into the ungrateful houseguest's hands.

"Hans, you truly are an angel!" Nate hugged the old queen before they hit the road. "Now, boys, in the trunk, I have outfits for us to change into."

"Outfits?" Beso asked as the orange BMW swerved onto

Crescent Heights Boulevard. "What's wrong with what I have on now?"

"Well, for one, it screams 'Banana Republic sale!' For another, Chapped Hide is a rough trade leather and fetish production company. I think that calls for something a bit butcher than plain-front khakis and a candy-cane striped polo!"

"Fine!" Beso crossed his arms and leaned back into the seat.

"I just love new outfits," Jorge raved. "Tell me, Nate, what do you have in store for us?"

"Well, once Hans began on breakfast, I took it upon myself to raid his closet."

"Dios mío!" Jorge spat in disgust, "I'm not wearing that old *puto*'s clothing. It's probably all boatneck sweaters and flared pants!"

"It was the best I could find in the shortest amount of time. Once we get over the hill, I'll pull off to the side of the road so we can all change."

As promised, once the trio had wound through Laurel Canyon, Nate pulled into the parking lot of a Von's grocery store and popped open his trunk.

"Assless chaps!" Beso screamed at the sight. "I can't wear *these!*"

"You *can* and you *will*," Nate said sternly. "Remember, boys, this is all for a good cause."

Completely changed into their new gear, the three completed the toilsome journey to Van Nuys. Off Victory Boulevard, they saw a small, hastily carved wooden paddle with the words "Chapped Hide" burned into the makeshift sign. A small, twisted arrow pointed the way toward a dark alleyway. Pulling into the parking lot, Beso gasped. "Nate, look!"

By the entrance of the parking lot was the same blue van that had carried Myles Long's abductors! Before Nate could respond, a large, burly, and hairy redhead clad in old blue jeans and a leather vest leapt out of the van, stubbing his cigar with a boot heel on the blacktop. From behind a pair of biker-cop sunglasses, the man stared the three down.

Beso slid as deeply into the bucket seat as space would allow. "I told you this was a bad idea."

"Well hello, boys," the leather daddy bellowed. "I've been *waiting* for you!"

LIVES ON THE LINE

"Oh, you've been waiting for us, have you?" Beso challenged, suddenly summoning up his courage.

"Well, actually," the leather daddy explained, removing his biker cop sunglasses to reveal a pair of gentle green eyes, "I've been waiting for *you*." It took Nate a second to respond—when he realized the man was looking directly at him.

"Why, yes! And…it's good to meet you as well. But I'm sorry, I don't recognize—"

The leather daddy scoffed before extending his hand. "I'm Guy Carley, Daddy Guy, if you please. I'm the fluffer and production assistant on this shoot. And I definitely know who you are. Although, I must say, you look even better in person!"

"Is that a fact?" Nate leaned comfortably against the side of his convertible.

"Trust me, I've seen every Rhett Rosebud film. We're all very honored to have you on this shoot here at Chapped Hide."

"Rhett Rosebud," Nate repeated, baffled yet buying time. "Why yes, Daddy Guy, it's great to meet you. I'm honored to be here as well."

"And who is this you've brought along?" Guy inquired.

"My entourage," Nate said, glazing over the details. "I never leave home without them."

"I have to say," Guy admitted, "I was a bit thrown off by the blaze orange BMW you're driving. Not what I saw you tooling around in, in town at all!"

"We use this to throw off my fans," the newly christened Rhett Rosebud explained, running an affectionate finger over the hood of his cherished convertible. "It may not be as butch as a dark blue late-model, blocked-window van. But it will have to do."

"This old thing?" Guy tapped the side of the van. "They sure don't make 'em like they used to!"

"I'll say," Jorge supported. "Looks just like one we saw over in West Hollywood yesterday. That one was a real beaut, too!"

"But that couldn't have been the same one," Beso continued. "Daddy Guy wasn't behind the wheel!"

Guy's brow furrowed as he spoke. "Probably was. Loaned it to a friend of mine yesterday."

"That explains it!" Nate's eyes brightened. "The driver did look familiar. I almost want to say it was that hunk from Tucci Productions, Buck Steers."

"Sorry to say it was," Guy sneered. "He must have returned it sometime in the middle of the night, left the keys in the ignition. Would you believe the stud didn't even have the manners to fill up the gas tank?"

"The nerve!" Nate was relieved to have questions regarding the van answered. "Guy, if you don't mind, I have a few details to work out with my friends before I get started today. Mind giving us some alone time?"

Guy stepped into the studio and Nate turned to his two pals, his eyes glowing with excitement. "The coincidence is unreal! He actually thinks I'm the star of the film they're shooting. And here I was, worried about how I was going to get in."

"Nate," Beso challenged, "Do you have any idea who Rhett Rosebud *is*?"

"While my catalog of porn stars and their careers is somewhat impressive, I must admit the name barely rings a bell. But how bad can he be?"

"Well, you'll be putting your ass on the line," Jorge warned. "Rhett Rosebud may be the fresh freckle-faced, redheaded porn star that you bear a striking resemblance to. However, he is also quite *famoso* for something else."

Nate looked at the two blankly.

Beso exclaimed, "Even *I* know this! Rhett's only in *fisting films*."

"What?" Nate's face grew pale.

"His big debut was in *The Last Puppeteer*. Since then, he's been in several, including *Pirate's Booty*. That's the one I saw him in. Summer pre-work for my Gay Pop Culture class," Beso explained. "Let's put it this way: he has an *insatiable* appetite. Or at least one particular part of his anatomy does!"

Guy stepped out from the studio doorway. "We're ready when you are, Rosebud!"

"Be—right—there!" Nate said with false confidence.

Only Beso and Jorge detected the wavering in his tone.

"This is gonna be your best pic yet," Guy said, smoking a newly lit cigar. "Believe me when I say that *A Farewell to Forearms* is definitely going to be blockbuster material!" Smiling, he leaned back in and closed the door.

"*A—Farewell—to…*" Nate closed his eyes and shuddered.

Regaining his determination, he stood up straight and flashed his eyes.

"I'm *doing this*. It might provide the only lead we have on Myles Long!"

"Are you sure you're ready?" Jorge asked.

"I have to be." The redhead grabbed his book bag out of the trunk of the car. "I need you two to stay out here. When Rhett Rosebud really arrives, tell him the shoot's been rescheduled for tomorrow. In the meantime, I'll do everything I can to find out as much about Myles Long as possible."

Beso and Jorge reluctantly agreed to the scheme. "Nate, if you aren't back in thirty minutes, we're storming the studio!" Beso warned.

"Make it forty-five. I'm going to buy as much time as I can before they begin shooting."

Nate stepped to the front of the studio, its white siding covered with graffiti and eroded from years of neglect. Before he could knock on the door, it swung open and Guy greeted him, smiling, the cigar clenched between his teeth. The studio lobby was empty, save for an oscillating fan that click-clicked in motion upon a metal desk top. Head shots of numerous men lined the right side wall. Some were yellowed with age; a few peeled and even curled at edges. One of those immediately caught Nate's attention. At the top, just off-center, was a photo of a man identical to the man who had attempted to abduct him during Myles Long's boynapping!

"All these stars!" Nate mused, "Some look *so* familiar, but it's just been so long."

"Chapped Hide has been around almost twenty years," Guy boasted, pointing at a photo in the far left corner. "Even I had my place in the sun once."

Nate admired the photo of Guy, much younger, with a full head of hair, the same gentle green eyes, and an expression both enthusiastic and naïve. "You looked great! You still do!"

"This is a tough field," Guy explained, "especially when you're a bottom. Trust me, Rhett, we're a dime a dozen in this business."

"I guess I'm just riding the wave," Nate explained.

"Well!" Guy laughed. "You do have an extra ability that could keep you famous for years to come. I don't know how you do it!"

"Neither do I." Nate was growing more apprehensive by the moment. He shifted his attention to the man in the off-center photo. Though it was taken years ago, he still recognized the close-cropped dark-shaved head, the olive skin and hairy biceps—from the parking lot kidnapping. What Nate recognized most, however, were the dark piercing eyes, which momentarily made him forget to breathe. Even in the aged photo, it was as though the eyes were looking directly into his!

"Who's this? He looks familiar, but I can't place..."

Guy's cheerful expression suddenly changed. "That's Mac Needles."

Nate remembered what Phil Templeton had said to Jorge: *You gotta know better than to cross Mac.*

"Don't recognize the name." Each time Nate glanced at the photo, he could feel his mouth grow dry. His heartbeat pounded with a heavy thud.

"May I have a glass of water, Guy?"

The fluffer walked to a water cooler by the desk and filled a tall paper cup for Chapped Hide's newest star. "Mac hasn't been in a movie for a long time. He's from the mid-eighties, my own time. When the company first began. He was kind of a hell-raiser at the time, and a few of the big investors asked him to stay away."

"Where's he now?" Nate attempted to feign only a moderate interest. He found his grip weak when he took the cup from Guy's hand. The sight of Mac Needles had drained him of the false bravado he'd summoned up in the parking lot.

"No one knows," Guy replied. "Some of these guys on this wall just...vanished! Now and then, someone runs into them at a coffee shop, or in a Laundromat." He paused sadly. "Then weeks later you hear that someone had a funeral you never knew of. I guess that's what happens. After all, twenty years is a long time!"

"You've been here all that time?" Nate asked.

"I've left a few times," Guy explained. "But I always come back when I need money. Hate to say it, but this is almost like home for me."

Nate looked around the studio, trying to imagine the twenty years of activity that had taken place there. He turned his attention back to the wall photo. "It's just amazing to me, all these men you've known. And now, so many of them you'll never see again."

"Like I said, we cross paths now and then. Believe me, I have some stories I could tell you."

"Oh?"

"Some of them are kinda sad, really," the leather daddy said, stubbing out his second cigar of the day. "I still remember this one incident every now and then. It was Christmas 1991. I was making a huge dinner at my place for the orphans: you know, those friends and acquaintances that don't have any place to go for Christmas? Earlier that week, I'd invited my friend Roger and he'd agreed to bring homemade pies. The day of the dinner, however, he barely made it in time for dessert. Had those pies in his hands, but his face was flushed. He was all nervous."

"*Not* the normal holiday spirit?" Nate suggested.

"Exactly! So, after dessert, most of the other guests left to go home. Roger finally started to loosen up. A few eggnogs will do that. And I'll never forget it. I said, 'Rog, you look as if you've seen a ghost.'"

"What did he say?"

Guy looked up at the wall of photos and then back at Nate very solemnly. "He said, 'Guy, I not only *saw* a ghost, but think *I just slept* with *one.*' At that point, I sat down and he explained that he'd started his morning off on The Line, looking for a quickie before dinner."

"The Line?"

"Phone lines! Chat lines! This was before the Internet exploded. Aside from cruisy spots, The Line was probably the easiest way to get laid quickly."

"I see—a pre-Internet chat site."

"How it worked was, everyone left a message on the line, like an ad, about what they looked like and what they were looking *for*. You could skip to the next message or you could reply if an ad caught your attention. I should tell you, my friend Roger was extremely hot, I mean drop-dead gorgeous. If people say they only met sleaze queens on those lines, then they were on the wrong line. Roger was on there almost every day, and he was one of the most beautiful men I've known. He had a killer body, Statue of David quality, golden tan skin, and blond curly hair always tousled to perfection."

"Sounds hot." Nate was thinking of another beautiful blond with curly hair he had recently crossed paths with—Myles Long!

"And the brightest blue eyes! Great guy, too! Really big heart. He'd do anything for you. That's what got him into trouble that day," Guy reflected solemnly.

"What do you mean?"

"He met this guy over the phone. They chatted and really clicked. The trick was looking for everything Roger had—body, hair, eyes, butt—his ass was like two honeydews in August! Roger had spent hours on the phone looking for a decent trick. The Line was almost empty, on account of the holiday, and this guy was the only one who sounded at all decent. Kept asking all sorts of questions, really specific things that he wanted."

"Like…"

"Roger said it was almost like setting up a certain scene the guy was into…The guy said he wanted him to be completely silent, no talking at all when he came in, and none when the two of them were about to make it. He kept asking Roger if he liked to kiss, until finally Roger was like, 'Enough already! Either we meet, or I'm jacking off—before my pies burn!'"

"So they finally met." Nate was finding himself consumed by the details of Guy's story.

"When Roger first entered the trick's apartment—a little studio in Silverlake—the lights were dim, there were lit candles everywhere. Another crazy detail, *The Carpenters Christmas* cassette was playing in the background. He recognized the guy a little, but thought maybe from the gym, or a bar. When he tried to look at the man too closely, the trick backed away, his face disappearing into the room's shadows.

"But, as I said, their agreement had been for no talking whatsoever. The man greeted Roger with a hug and they promptly began to make out. Roger slept with just about everyone he crossed paths with, but he swore it was the most intimate make-out session he had ever had. Each kiss became deeper and more seductive, and this guy's hold on Roger stronger and more controlling as he guided him to the bed in the corner of the studio.

"He found himself so locked into the sudden heat of their encounter that he couldn't recall the build-up to this man actually getting inside him. Once he was in, the trick completely took control, his cock plunging deeply, and then pulling halfway out, but never allowing Roger to rest. The sensation of this man inside him had a primal feeling, one that made Roger succumb to the sudden notion that this was what he'd been searching for all along. It was as if it was either this man's first or last time, and he was going to prolong his climax until Roger completely broke. Needless to say, Roger said the lovemaking was the most overwhelmingly intense experience he'd ever known. Or ever would know…" Guy's voice trailed off dreamily.

"What's so disturbing about that?" Despite the pressing reality of his manhunt, the amateur detective couldn't help but acknowledge the gradual awakening that was occurring within him as the tale unraveled.

"Keep in mind, this was a Christmas trick, and Roger still had somewhere to be for dinner. By the time they were in bed, with this trick holding him tight, he realized how lonely the guy was. I still remember what Roger said: 'It was almost as if he was trying to replace someone in his life. Using me.'"

"That makes sense. Especially as he was so specific about what type he wanted."

"But what happened after they'd finished having sex was what left Roger so disturbed. The longer they were together, the more he could sense a strong pull of need in the man. His dark eyes seemed so hollow! He'd look at Roger, then gaze away. As Roger got up to leave, thanking him for the good time, the guy grabbed him firmly by the arm. Then he blurted out, 'Don't leave me again!' and began to cry."

"How sad!"

"Roger didn't know what to do. He held the man as long as he could, but he wouldn't stop crying. The candles were beginning to burn out and the room was silent, as the cassette had ended. Roger had never experienced such emptiness in anyone, especially considering how, only moments earlier, their lovemaking had been so filled with life and energy.

"Finally, the trick seemed to get it back together. But he couldn't even bring himself to look at Roger. 'You have to go,' was all he said. When Roger hesitated, the man turned and gave him so menacing a look that even hours later, it still left Roger shaken. He said he had never seen anything like it. He felt as though he was in the room with the Devil himself! Suddenly, the man pulled open the blinds that had darkened the room and glared coldly. 'Leave while you still can!' the man bellowed. It was then, as the late-winter sun washed into the room, that Roger realized this face he had been trying to place earlier belonged to none other than Mac Needles!"

Nate's gaze darted up to the dark eyes in the photo, the haunted stare taunting him as Guy revealed the last detail of his Christmas tale:

"Roger tore out of the apartment, hopped in his car, and never looked back." Guy rested on the desk chair and looked wearily at Nate. "He told me that if he hadn't left right then, at that very moment, he believed Mac Needles would have killed him!"

A FISTFUL OF HOLLERS!

Before Nate could ask more about Mac Needles, a stunning Italian with dark, wavy hair entered the studio. His form-fitting white T-shirt revealed the lithe muscles of a professional swimmer's build, tucked into tight worn blue jeans that were fully cupped in the crotch.

Glancing up at him, Nate could barely control himself before uttering in recognition, "Gino Rantelli!"

"You must be Rhett Rosebud." Gino smiled brightly, stepping forward and kissing Nate on the lips, his pencil-thin mustache tickling the *faux* star slightly. He draped his well-muscled arm along Nate's back, grabbing his butt with a warm hand.

"Good to finally meet you, I've heard so *much*. Together, you and I will make *A Farewell to Forearms* a surefire hit!"

Nate's cheeks colored with the recollection of how he'd gained access to the studio in the first place. "I am such a fan!" Nate gushed. "*The Straight Shooter* is one of my favorite films."

"Everyone's favorite this year—it seems." Gino glanced around the room. "Guy, where is everyone? I thought we were gonna try to get this all done in one day."

"Still waiting for a few calls, Gino, seems like everyone's running behind this morning. Don't worry, if no one else comes, I can operate the camera. The lighting, blocking, all that is set."

"I'm surprised you're working at Chapped Hide," Nate

continued. "I thought you were strictly contracted to Tucci Productions."

Gino scoffed, scratching his arm before raising one trademark eyebrow. Rantelli was in his mid-thirties but easily had the body of a twenty-year-old, and was one of the most famous stars in Tucci's house. While many would have cited his early blockbusters, Nate called upon his most recent act, a steamy scene with Myles Long.

In that movie, after the hot, erection-inducing elevator ride with Buck Steers, Myles manages to clean himself off and get to his office without too much difficulty. After making a few important business calls, Myles decides it's time to call his secretary and find out why his lunch is so late. To his relief, at that moment, his sandwich and salad arrive—with Gino Rantelli as the delivery boy. As might be expected from a ravenous businessman on a tight schedule, Long reads Gino the riot act. That is, of course, until his mind-reading abilities return and he realizes the delivery boy wants more than a tip for his services.

"I'll give you more than an eggplant panini," Gino thinks, "I'll give you the blow job of your life, too!"

Without hesitation, Myles unzips his pants and pops out his recently worked tool into the delivery boy's mouth.

"That was such a hot scene," Nate said admiringly as Guy proceeded to outfit him in a costume consisting of a dog collar and leather vest. He then led the two to the studio, a barren concrete stage with a large steel bench in the center of the room.

"Yes. Unfortunately, it's been my *only* scene in months," Gino complained sullenly. "The only one Tucci has any screen time for these days is Myles Long."

"I haven't seen the guy myself, but he's red hot right now, from what I hear," Guy agreed. "I wouldn't be surprised if Anitra created a separate production company centered solely around him."

Gino pointedly glared at Guy before rolling his eyes in exasperation.

"Okay," Guy said, taking the hint and quickly changing the subject, "you guys get yourselves settled. I'm gonna make a few phone calls and see where everyone's at. We gotta get this picture started. Neither of you are the cheap trade I'm used to having here!"

The kind-hearted Bear strode off the set and back into the office.

"And don't forget, I gotta be in Palm Springs tomorrow—for a dancing gig!" Gino chimed in.

"I see," Nate returned to their earlier topic, "so you decided to look for work at another house."

"Chapped Hide's always trying to get Tucci's stars. So I figured it would be the ultimate kiss-off if I moved here. Besides, this place may look like a dump, but what they don't pay out for upgrades and amenities, they definitely do pay for established actors." He shrugged humbly. "Hey, why am I explaining this to you? They must have paid a *mint* to get you here."

"It *was* a laborious contract negotiation," the redhead agreed. "I'm sure everyone asks, but I've got to know: what was it like, working with—"

"Myles Long?" The Italian glowered. "I'm so sick of hearing that prick's name. And to think I allowed him to put his cock in my mouth for a mere two grand! The whole idea makes me wanna vomit."

"Sorry. Bad topic," Nate apologized, although his curiosity was still piqued. "It sounds like Myles *is* the center of attention at Tucci. I knew he was popular, I just had no idea it was causing others so much grief."

"I hope all those Myles Long feature films give Tucci a heat rash!" The forgotten star glowered. "You don't know how it pissed me off to get a shoddy two grand for that pic while that good-for-nothing twink got a new Mercedes from Tucci! And here I am one of the ones who helped build her company up to what it's become." He relaxed, his eyes brightening with hope. "But I guess that's all in the past. Now that I'm at Chapped Hide,

I'll be calling the shots. The investors here are silent partners for the most part, so we on contract get to participate in the production. No more cheesy plots like Tucci's—we'll just have hot, raw sex—all the time!"

"Great!" Nate said, a bit falsely, before attempting a subtle segue. "I have to tell you, I was on holiday for the summer, so I'm not quite sure I'm entirely loosened up for the scene we're going to be shooting."

"No problem," Gino winked knowingly, "I'll be gentle. Although, from what I've seen of your films, you won't need any encouraging, you little Fist Piggy!"

Nate's face crimsoned as he looked at Rantelli's large, bulging wrist and the huge, marble-sized knuckles of his fingers. Clearly, casting Gino hadn't been based upon his swarthy Italian looks!

Leading Nate to the bench, Gino gently pushed his shoulders against the cold metal.

"We can get ready while we wait for the others," Gino suggested, turning his attention to a CD player next to the bench. "If you don't mind, I'd really like to play some heavy metal to get myself in the mood."

"Heavy metal?" Nate asked, barely able to cover his disgust.

"Can't explain it. It just about always gets me rock-hard. Better than any fluffer I've ever met."

The banging of drums and the angry screams of a hard rocker blasted from the studio as Guy scanned his list of phone numbers inside the office, frantically trying to locate his production crew for the shoot. From what he'd heard of Gino, the screeching of electric guitars and wail of a scratchy-voiced singer confirmed rumors of what got the Italian in the mood. Guy laughed as he dialed the number for the cameraman.

"Joe! Where you at?" Guy asked. "I've got Gino and Rhett Rosebud here and, trust me, these guys don't like to be kept waiting. We've gotta get this shoot done, or else." Guy slammed down the phone. If all else failed, he could do the camera work, but not the lights and sound, too. That would be such a hassle!

As he looked for the number of another cameraman, he heard the door to the production office open, and a light autumn breeze blew into the room. Without looking up, Guy sighed. "It's about *time* you got here. Here's a first: We've got the stars of the film waiting for the *production crew*! I've got news, sweetheart, your name ain't Lindsay Lohan!"

The man said nothing but stood silently before the desk. Looking up, Guy first made out the tight black leather pants and jacket. He gasped when he saw a face he'd not seen in years. A face so intense, so dark with fury, all Guy could do was let out a desperate scream. Backing from the desk, he made a move for the door. But the man blocked him, pushing him back against the wall, forcing his gloved hand against Guy's throat.

"No!" Guy gasped, but it was the only plea he could utter. The hard leather glove pressed against his throat as he struggled for air. His eyes watered. He tried to open them to the blurred vision of the man in front of him.

"Now you listen, you good-for-nothing fluffette! If you know what's good for you, you'll keep your overworked pie-hole shut." He pushed harder against Guy's throat.

Guy's eyes rolled into the back of his head and his face turned purple. With one final slam against Guy's neck, the man growled, "Got it?"

He released his hold and the Bear collapsed to the floor, his green eyes wide open in terror.

❖

"Now *that's* what I call a song!" Gino raved as the cut ended. He had one hand on his growing hard-on as he gently moved an index finger into Nate's hole. "I'm *definitely* ready for you, Rhett Rosebud. But where's everyone *else*?"

"That's a good question." Nate was too distracted by his upcoming role to think of much else.

Annoyed, Gino paused the next track of the CD and ripped off the latex glove he'd been wearing, then stepped into the office. "Guy, what the hell is…"

Nate followed right behind him. They rushed behind the desk, where they found the Bear still on the floor, his eyes glazed over. A breeze swung the door fully open, hitting the office wall. Gino cradled Guy's head as Nate frantically dialed 911, only to realize the phone line had been cut!

Grabbing his cell phone from the studio, Nate made the call. Within minutes, the paramedics arrived, and then Jorge and Beso also rushed in, panic-stricken.

"Thank God you're all right," the cousins cried.

"Did you see who did this?" one paramedic asked Nate and Gino.

"No," Nate uttered, then added in a lower voice, "but I think I know who it was." They tried to bring the victim back to consciousness. Nate rushed to the wall of photos he'd earlier seen, during his arrival.

The photo of Mac Needles was gone! Torn off the wall! The only remains were a small corner piece of the yellowed shot hanging by a staple.

PART TWO: MAC NEEDLES

NEEDLES IN A HAYSTACK

"And *that*, my friends, is what happened inside the studio."
Nate sipped on a much-needed Cosmo at The Tavern.

"*Increíble*, Nate!" Jorge said, "We're lucky you're even alive!"

"I told you guys this was a bad idea," Beso reminded them, flagging the bartender down for a second white wine spritzer. "I knew the minute I got into those chaps that we were headed for *big* trouble."

"I'll say," Jorge replied, laughing. "The real Rhett Rosebud? He took one look at us in our get-ups and he practically ran in the other direction."

"He thought we were crazed fans!" Beso chortled along with his cousin, "He was all, like, 'No! No autographs, please!'"

"I'm glad you kept him out of the studio so I was able to find out what I could," Nate replied. "Clearly, boys, this was a worthwhile trip." For all of them, however, the memory of Guy being rushed to the hospital did spoil the mood a smidge. They hoped the friendly fluffer would survive the attack. "I'm convinced Mac Needles was Daddy Guy's attacker. And for him to strike like that so soon again means we're getting even closer to finding Myles Long!"

"Are you sure this is a *good* sign?" Beso asked. "Nate! We don't want you to end up like that fluffer any more than we wanted you to end up like Rhett Rosebud!" He leaned back and sipped his cocktail before he smiled at Nate, licking his lips. "Speaking of which, just how much did you have to *stretch* to accommodate this new role?"

"I'll have you know, my dear Beso, that my *culo*, as Jorge calls it, is still tight as a drum. And," the young redhead declared, defiantly, "I'd put my *culo* on the line again, too, if it meant finding another clue on Myles Long's kidnapping."

"And you really think it's because he fits a type that Mac Needles has a weakness for?" Beso asked, still uncertain.

"Yes," Nate said with measured confidence. "Well built, blue-eyed, curly-haired blond boys."

"With a dick that can split two-by-fours in one measured whack!" Beso added, "You forgot that!"

"Well, if this Mac *is* obsessed with hot blonds," Jorge fanned himself in relief, "thank heavens I'm brown as a *café con leche!*"

Beso nodded. "And praise the Lord that I'm big, brown, and sweaty, 'cause now there's *no way* this Needle is coming *anywhere* near my haystack!"

"All right, Beso," Nate said, "no more cocktails for you." He eyed the shirtless bartender in the distance. "Check, please!"

The bartender sashayed slowly over to the trio with a smirk. "All your drinks have been taken care of," he explained, nodding behind the boys. The three turned at once and came face-to-face with Miss Anitra Tucci.

"Yes, Deke," Anitra smiled lustily at the hunky bartender, "just put all those cocktails on my tab."

"Why, Anitra!" Nate said. "What a pleasant surprise!"

"Thank you for the cocktails." Beso promptly put his wallet back in his book bag.

"Actually, I was about to call you, Nate. So it's fortuitous you've arrived for happy hour," she explained. "Is there any chance we could chat in my office? While I buy your two friends here another round?"

"In *that* case, you can have him for as long as you *need*." Beso pushed his empty glass forward, snapping his fingers to get Deke's attention. "What harm can a few more white wine spritzers do?"

"Hopefully less than it did *last night*," Jorge said, at which Beso narrowed his eyes before perking up at the delivery of his favorite drink.

"I'll be right back, boys," Nate said as he followed Anitra to a small flight of stairs to the right of the restrooms. Skylights along the walk washed the white melamine-paneled aisle with a bright, alabaster glow, leading to a large frosted-glass door.

"I had no idea all this existed," Nate said as they strode the hallway.

"Not only is The Tavern just one part of my large empire, it also serves as my headquarters," Tucci boasted, waving Nate into her palatial office. "In fact, I must say I have discovered many a star right here! What many may think was a slow Monday night for The Tavern, might, in fact, have been a *very busy* one for Tucci Productions," she said.

Nate took in the room's stark, modern appearance. Varying shades of pale gray and off-white dominated the room. To the left, a wall of flat-screen televisions displayed different angles of activity within The Tavern.

Along the other wall was a cocktail bar with theatre-sized posters promoting Tucci's latest features, one of which was *The Straight Shooter*.

Pausing momentarily before the bar, Nate looked up at the poster, an artist's rendering of Myles Long, his left arm elevated to a basketball hoop, completing a perfect rim-shot. On each side of the portrait were clips from scenes in the movie, painted in the same careful brushstrokes. "Now, Nate," Anitra asked as she slid behind her desk into a soft white leather chair, "is there *anything* I could get you to drink?"

The sudden reality of being alone again with this high-powered woman, this time invited into her office, caught Nate off guard. The detailed care with which everything was placed, from the perfectly symmetrical mounting of the flat screens to the skintight fit of Tucci's canary yellow business suit, made Nate feel as though he was in a Tucci Production himself. Sinking slowly into the white leather Barcelona chair opposite the desk, Nate realized the world he was entering had been created by that same well-disciplined eye for detail that made the producer's films so successful. Crossing one leg and looking at Anitra as she smiled, he slowly took in the surroundings, allowing himself to be enveloped—if only briefly—by a fantasy world. "Oh, I'll have whatever *you're* having," he replied, still soaking in the moment.

Tucci pressed the intercom at her desk. "Mario, please bring me a bottle of Dom and two flutes," she purred before releasing the button. "You know, Nate, the more I've thought about it, the more curious I am about your obsession with my latest film."

"I wouldn't say it's an obsession," Nate said dreamily, staring at the movie poster just to his right. "I just enjoyed every minute of *The Straight Shooter*."

"And you'd enjoy every inch of its star, Myles Long, I also presume." Tucci gazed at him knowingly.

Her intuitive statement knocked Nate out of his dream-state and he shifted suddenly in his seat, now fully entangled in her gaze.

She continued to study him until Mario entered with a bottle of champagne. "Perfect timing!" Anitra said as he uncorked it with a sound like a gunshot. "I propose a toast," she said softly, as Mario left the room, "To *new friends*."

"New friends," Nate agreed cautiously, wishing his *old friends* were with him at that moment. On the far left monitor, he watched the bar as Beso and Jorge laughed over cocktails, then he turned his attention back to Tucci. "The meeting with Myles at school, that was a chance encounter. I'm just doing the same for him as I would for *anyone* who was abducted."

"I'm sure." Tucci stared at the bubbles floating to the top of her crystal flute. "Listen, Nate, it's no mystery Myles Long has a strong fan-base, but I have to be cautious when porn star worship reaches the point of obsession. That's where *my* concern comes in," she said with finality as she leaned forward, her French-manicured fingers folded atop the desk.

"I understand that completely," Nate stammered, his hand shaking a bit as he sipped what was left of the champagne. "But if you're saying I had anything to do with Myles Long's abduction…"

"No," her tone softened, "I'm not referring to *your* obsession. I know enough about you to believe your desire for my top star is nothing more than harmless lust."

"You know enough about me?" Nate asked, surprised.

"You're not the only one who does investigating, Mr. Dainty." Tucci refilled their glasses. "I always do a thorough background check before I proverbially get into bed with anyone, *on* or *off* camera."

"I guess you'd have to," Nate reasoned, "to protect yourself and your business."

"After our meeting yesterday, I needed to know whether or not I could trust you. I asked you to come up here because of something I discovered on my desk when I came into work this morning."

"Something that makes you think Myles was abducted by an obsessed fan?"

"You could say that," Tucci said evenly. She moved to the side of the desk and lifted a white padded envelope, removing a DVD and holding it up with one hand. "I asked you here so you could see for yourself."

Kneeling below the panel of televisions, she slid open a long glass cabinet, revealing a wide variety of video and DVD players.

"That's some electronics collection!" Nate squinted to make

out, in particular, one beast of a tape deck in the far corner, whirring and humming as though in its final moments of life. "The one on the far end sounds just about done for."

Anitra leaned back and checked the cabinet in question before moving closer and rubbing the top of the old machine. "This old Betamax? I remember when this player used to purr like a kitten." She shrugged. "It's probably the last of its kind in L.A."

"I can see why," Nate said. Tucci inserted the DVD into a more modern, much less noisy player. Immediately, images from The Tavern disappeared, and every television screen lit up.

Nate leaned forward to a low buzzing from the surround sound at the video's start. The grainy image of a wooded area at night was a sharp contrast to the well lit, sharply executed, Tucci Productions. As the cameraman led them through the wooded area stumbling and swerving along the poorly kept path, title letters rolled on the screen: *Tough to Snuff*. From deep in the background, they could hear a muffled cry as the camera came upon Myles Long, his arms tied around the back of a large oak, his legs pinned to the sides of its trunk. He was completely naked, save for a handkerchief that covered his mouth. The camera slowly trailed along the star's body, stopping at small bruises and cuts all over his torso.

"Those marks weren't there when I saw him at school." Nate realized how much the star must have been through in the past twenty-four hours.

From behind the camera suddenly appeared a sharp knife held by a gloved hand. Myles' muffled grunts grew louder as the knife approached, brushing his midsection. Nate turned away as the knife slowly cut into the young star, the pain evidenced by his gagged cries, then sudden silence. When he turned back to the televisions, the words *To Be Continued...* were emblazoned on the screens before flickering out.

Tucci clicked off the player and turned to Nate. He set what was left of his champagne down.

"Now, am I correct in my understanding of the title, *Tough to Snuff*?" Nate asked the producer.

"I'm afraid you are. A snuff film is typically one that depicts a murder or suicide, and is typically perversely pornographic in nature. Obviously, such movies are illegal. But from what I hear, there's quite an underground demand for them by fetishists."

Anitra poured herself what was left of the champagne and walked to the window. "Let's face it, having Myles Long as a star for this kind of movie would be equivalent to winning the lottery."

"This is more serious than I imagined," Nate groaned.

Tucci agreed. "If we don't do something soon, it will be too late." She stood and walked out to the office's small balcony, gazing at the activity on San Vicente Boulevard. "I know Chapped Hide well enough to know that *they* would never take things this far. This is someone else's work."

Nate looked at the adult entertainment tycoon, lost in thought, dread crossing her face. Despite the traumatic conflict he'd witnessed on-screen, Nate wondered if perhaps he was now living another well-rehearsed scene of Anitra Tucci's life. Was the sense of fear that now filled the room a feeling she'd worked to set up and perfect—for his arrival? Still uncertain of her motives, Nate decided to keep his adventure at Chapped Hide to himself.

"At this point, Nate," Tucci turned to the redhead, "I'm going to have to involve the police. Much as I hate to see the press have a heyday with this situation, it's more important we get Myles Long back at Tucci Productions." A small, heavily mascara-ed tear slid down her thick foundation.

"I couldn't agree more." Despite his suspicions, Nate still found himself moved by her tender moment. "In the meantime, my friends and I will continue to do what we can to help find him, as soon as possible."

They parted ways and Nate rushed back to the bar to fill in Beso and Jorge on his recent discovery. To his disappointment, the duo was missing from the bar. Deke eyed him and explained,

"They're at the Internet café wing. Cruising the chat rooms, I'm sure."

Nate entered the Internet café and breathed in the aroma of fresh-roasted coffee. The slow tempo of bossa nova music provided a contrast to the fast beat playing in the rest of The Tavern. In back of the café, hovering over a flat screen monitor, Nate found his friends, who waved him over excitedly. "Nate! You've gotta see this," Jorge's right deltoid flexed as he leaned toward the keyboard.

"This is dreadful!" Beso said, between bites of a white chocolate macadamia nut cookie. "We looked up Mac Needles on Gaypornipedia.com, and much to my disgust, there's a clip of him jacking off!"

"Aw, he's just sore 'cause he recognizes a *certain part* of Mac Needles more than he would like to." Jorge clicked on Play to show Nate the loop. The computer displayed Needles lying back in a chair, wearing black boots and black gloves, the rest of him naked and well-oiled. Nate watched as Mac's left hand slowly slid down his hairy body to his groin, stroking his large, veiny cock in a long, drawn-out motion.

"That's the one!" Beso pointed at the screen confidently. "That's the cock I sucked at the glory hole!"

❖

Watching traffic from the balcony, Anitra held the phone impatiently as she only half listened to the voice at the other end of the line. "It's a lost cause, darling," she hissed in response. "How many times do I have to tell you: your usefulness has passed!"

Grabbing a freshly opened bottle of champagne from the ice bucket, she filled her glass with a roll of the eyes. "I've had just about enough of your ridiculous threats! I'm untouchable, darling, and you know it!" She clicked the phone off with an air of finality and watched as the neon-lit skyline took bloom in the early night.

Suddenly, the lights of Tucci's office clicked off, leaving her in a shroud of darkness. "Damn automatic timers!" She walked back into the office to correct the situation and she realized that she wasn't alone. "Mario?"

A tall dark figure, clothed in black, stood at the entrance of her office. She froze at the sight of the intruder.

"Who's there?" she called, moving back slowly to the balcony.

The intruder moved closer, the top half of his face covered by a mask. She continued to back away, her questions growing more intense. "Who are you? What do you want?"

He lunged toward her with a broad leap, pushing her body against the balcony. Holding on for her life, Tucci grasped the railing and turned her head to the side, catching a quick glimpse of the traffic below. "Please, no," she begged. The wind picked up and blew her hair across her face. Her neck snapped back to face the attacker, freeing one hand up to remove the mask.

Growling, he pushed her away, her body crashing against the metal rails of the balcony. Rolling over, she stood up, kicked off her stilettos, and bolted for the door, determined to catch up with the man. But upon entering the hallway, she found that the intruder had completely vanished!

VOICES FROM THE PAST

Nate eyed the monitor with great curiosity. "Hold on! There must be more info about Mac Needles than just a j.o. video!" He took the mouse from Jorge and scanned to the side of the page where a small biography appeared.

Mac Needles (1961–?) was one of the great and now nearly forgotten gay film stars of the early 1980s. Although his dark, masculine good looks, mustache and hairy body often put him in the popular "Clone" category of that era, Mac's close-cropped hair, tattoos and his primarily silent screen presence set him apart from others, and he is often used as a model for many of the "rough trade" stars popular today.

An early discovery of porn pioneer James Robinson, Needles first appeared in a silent loop directed by Robinson in 1979. The popularity of that loop propelled him into the porn mainstream, resulting in his first full length feature: "Winner Takes All" (Tempest Productions, 1980) under the name Mack Needles. By 1981, he'd dropped the "K" in his name and starred in "Through a Needles' Eyes," which featured him in every scene, and was filmed the weekend of the star's 20th birthday. Other movies quickly followed, including "Bound and Determined" (Tempest Productions, 1982) and "Man Overboard" (Grease Monkey, 1983). Needles' popularity was just beginning to skyrocket, and several imitators, posing as brothers or cousins, appeared throughout the industry, including Jack Needles (billed as Mac's older and nastier brother), Lou Needles (a silver fox billed as Mac's orally fixated cousin) and a short-lived comedian from the gay circuit, Crack Needles (a doped-up, raging leather-daddy prone to crying jags). Although the star power of these wannabes never eclipsed Mac Needles' initial success, it did impact his bargaining power with producers and his popularity waned during the period of 1983–84.

In late 1985, Mac resurfaced with his "Bound and Determined" costar, Chase Hastings, with their new production company, Desert Heat Productions. Although the release of their upcoming film, "Magic Afternoon" (1986?), was heavily discussed and anticipated, the film was left incomplete following Hastings' sudden death in July 1986. In 1987, Mac had a cameo appearance as a correctional officer in Chapped Hide's "Death Row Orgy" and was slated to make a comeback under the company's new "rough trade" releases. After his cameo in "Orgy," however, Needles disappeared from the industry.

A variety of stories have surfaced regarding his whereabouts over the ensuing twenty years. Some claimed he was one of the many adult film stars of that time who succumbed to the AIDS epidemic. Others said the star was living quietly with his lover, running a café in Barcelona, Spain. Some have even claimed they slept with someone who looked like Needles would look aged, in bathhouses all across the country. The most frequently heard speculation was offered by his original producer, James Robinson, who in a 1998 interview alluded to the fact that Mac had been one of the first "gay for pay" actors and who said he was living in the Midwest with a wife and three kids, and running a used car dealership.

"If they only knew," Nate said as he scanned the article, clicking Play to view the five-minute loop of Needles once again. The camera was focused tight on Needles' face. Though his eyes were still dark and penetrating, they did appear to be warmer and more welcoming as the camera panned out to feature his well-toned physique. Needles eyed the camera in a teasing, taunting way that seemed to contradict Guy's story of the broken man his friend had claimed to encounter during that sad Christmas day fling.

"He looks as though he's enjoying himself," Nate commented as he watched Needles stretching, smirking sexily, tugging on his hard-on. There was no denying the man's hotness, Nate thought as he realized his own cock was stiffening in response.

"So, what do you think happened to this bro?" Jorge pondered. "Here, he doesn't look like such a bad guy."

"I'm afraid looks *can* be deceiving." Nate pried his eyes from the screen and revealed the details of his meeting with Tucci. "If Mac Needles is Myles Long's abductor, it looks like he's going to use him in an underground snuff film."

"How disgusting." Beso almost spat out his cookie. "I absolutely hate all types of tobacco, but chewing it is just gross!"

"Nah, silly." Jorge brushed the crumbs off his cousin's shirt. "Nate's saying Myles' abductors are planning to kill him and videotape it."

"Tucci's calling the police about the DVD she received," Nate continued, "but obviously we need all hands on deck and we have to do what we can to save Myles Long, before it's too late."

"Nate," Jorge said as he scanned the Internet page on

Needles one last time, "have you ever heard the name Chase Hastings before? Maybe this *hombre*'s death triggered his psycho behavior. Let's see what this dude Hastings looks like." Jorge typed the name *Chase Hastings* into the search engine and came up with a brief listing:

Chase Hastings (1963–1986) was a gay film star of the early 1980s who starred in the film "Bound and Determined" (Tempest Productions, 1982) with Mac Needles. Originally from Cincinnati, Ohio, Hastings arrived in Los Angeles in 1980 to spend the summer with his aunt in the Hancock Park area.

While cruising West Hollywood's "Vaseline Alley," he met Mac Needles, who was on his way to a photo-shoot with early porn director James Robinson. After appearing in a few of the director's loops, Hastings decided to make L.A. his permanent home. Hastings' boyish good looks (his first film was shot when he was 17) and similarity to mainstream actors of the time like Christopher Atkins and Allen Fawcett set him up for definite stardom.

After "Bound and Determined," Hastings left for Mexico in an attempt to make his name crossing over into Spanish telenovelas. His poor Spanish-language abilities (producers complained tirelessly of his thick Midwestern accent) and failure to show up for rehearsals made the young hunk's Mexican film career short-lived. Back in Los Angeles, Hastings struggled to make a comeback. In 1985, he formed a production company with Needles, Desert Heat Productions, and was given top billing in the film "Magic Afternoon" (1986). Before the film was completed, Hastings' sudden death resulted in the dissolution of the new company.

"And, of course, there's not one photo!" Beso said as he scanned the page.

"There is one. But only of his headstone." Jorge scrolled up and down. "You read the part where it said he was comparable to Christopher Atkins. I've seen that *Blue Lagoon* movie a few times, and the dude had some kinky-ass curls!"

"Very good, Jorge," Nate said. "I remember him in a movie with pirates and there were striking similarities between Atkins and Myles Long. If you ask me, though, Myles is much better looking!"

"It would help if we could get a picture of Chase Hastings other than this *pinche* tombstone," Jorge said in disgust.

"Hold a minute, Jorge." Nate brightened with discovery, "Let's see what we can find out about the producer who discovered Needles *and* Hastings: James Robinson."

Jorge typed the name in the Gaypornipedia site and came up with a bio:

> **James Robinson (1951–1999)** was an early, prolific contributor to the birth of gay adult film. Originally a producer of the "loop" films popular in the 1970s, Robinson is best known for his discovery of stars Mac Needles, Rawn Casper and Chase Hastings. As the production of gay adult films became more elaborate, Robinson's presence moved out of the spotlight up until a fascinating December 1998 interview, highlighting his early years in the field. A biography was said to be in the works, but never came out. Robinson was found dead in his Los Feliz apartment just weeks after the interview, the cause of his death listed as accidental asphyxiation.

"So much for *that* lead." Jorge scanned the article one last time.

"I think it's time for us to let the police take over," Beso chimed in, motioning for the others to get up. Other patrons were waiting to use the computer.

They exited the café into the cool early autumn night.

"And let Myles Long die in the process?" Nate challenged. "I don't think so, Beso!"

"Yeah, cousin! Get some *cojones* for a change," Jorge said. "We've got to help Nate out on this!"

"Here's what I think," Nate said as they hopped into the car. "We've gathered more information on Myles Long as we've crossed paths with his former costars, first Buck Steers, then Gino Rantelli at Chapped Hide. In sequence of the film, the next costar in line would be Manny Manos."

"Ooh, I love Manny Manos," Jorge said as he sat up at attention. "That *Straight Shooter* movie is a bit long and drawn-out. But that scene where Myles Long gets picked up at the car wash is Aitch O Tee hot!"

"Hopefully he has a passion for something a bit bolder than designing websites," Beso teased his virile cousin.

"Trust me, boys," Jorge promised, "I'll probe this part of the mystery with every inch of my *pinga*."

"Glad to hear it, Jorge, because I'd like you and Beso to track Manos down. I'm hoping the interactions Myles had with his costar will help lead us to his whereabouts."

"After all," Beso added, "It was Buck Steers who mentioned Mac in the first place."

"Now you're getting the point," Nate said excitedly. "I'm thinking that as production continued, there were more encounters with Mac Needles that his costars were aware of and thought were harmless—at the time!"

"What will you be doing while we're putting our lives on the line, Nate Dainty, studying Calculus?" Beso challenged as the trio drove back to the Dainty home.

"Once I drop you two off at Jorge's car, I'm going to head

to Cedars-Sinai Hospital to bring a certain patient in ICU some much needed roses."

"Daddy Guy," Beso said with realization. "He still thinks you're Rhett Rosebud!"

"And for the sake of this investigation, I'm going to have to stay in that role for one last visit. If Guy knows anything else about Mac's obsession with blonds, it will get us a step closer to Myles Long!"

Nate turned into the garage, surprised to see the doorway to the kitchen slightly ajar. "That's strange! Hans *never* leaves the door open. He's always telling me to keep it closed, especially at this time of year." As they stepped into the kitchen, they heard a low moan from below.

Switching on the lights, they found the aging houseboy lying in a pool of blood!

WHISPERS IN THE DARK!

Hans! Are you all right?" Nate knelt at Hans' side. "Can you hear me?"

The houseboy moaned before slowly opening his eyes. "Oh, Nathan! Thank heavens it's you."

Jorge stepped back to Beso. "Let that be a lesson to you, Beso. Always send an up-to-date and real photo of yourself on the Internet, or else you're bound to piss someone off, too."

"Jorge!" Nate lifted the houseboy up and helped him to his feet. Jorge arched one eyebrow knowingly, then proceeded to search the house to make sure the attacker was gone. With Beso's help, Nate assisted Hans to a chair in the breakfast nook and quickly got a towel and bag of ice for the cut that ran along the houseboy's shoulder.

"How on earth did this happen?" Beso asked, alarmed.

"I'm still in a daze over the sequence of events," Hans said slowly, taking a glass of water from Beso. "What I can tell you, for sure, Nathan, is that the man who attacked me was looking for *you*!"

"Let me guess," Beso said, "Was he tall, dark and menacing?"

"Oh, *por favor*." Jorge reentered the breakfast nook. "Don't try making *your trick gone bad* look like some sort of brutal attack, Hans. I just walked into the living room to see you were cruising on Mantramp.com and had already given a trick this address!"

"That's just a coincidence," the houseboy insisted weakly as he held his shoulder. "In fact, at first, I thought this man *was* the guy I'd met on Mantramp! There was definitely something familiar about him. Unfortunately, he only wanted one thing."

"Let me guess," Jorge chided. "It *wasn't* one of your famous pineapple pancakes."

"It just so happens, George, he was searching for your good friend, Nathan." Hans regained his ability to snap back. He turned to the redhead and continued his explanation: "The moment I opened the door—and understand I was expecting a very different kind of encounter—my attacker pushed me to the wall and began to demand I tell him where you were!"

"Was he tall, dark and menacing, as Beso described him?" Nate asked.

"I would have to say—yes. Menacing isn't even the word. He was just evil! After he pushed me against the wall, he practically strangled me, and then knocked me onto the floor." The houseboy burst into tears. "Oh Nathan! I was so scared! So scared for you! I don't know what your uncle Carter would do if I let anything happen to you. We have to call the police and tell them."

"We will," Nate agreed. "But first I'm going to take you to the hospital to make sure you're all right."

"I'll make sure everything's locked and the lights are off," Jorge volunteered. "Hans, would you like me to leave a note for your trick, to let him know you'd like to take a rain check?"

"That's enough, Jorge!" Beso whispered, "Can't you see Hans might have really gotten hurt?"

After gathering up a small Vuitton overnight bag for the stricken houseboy, Nate and Beso helped him into the car. Certain the house was secure, Jorge returned with a small matchbox in his hands.

"Hey guys, does this belong to any of you?" He held the

matchbook out for everyone to see: a small, thin pale blue box, with the word *Sueños* written across the top.

They shook their heads. Sliding it open, Jorge saw an address and phone number listed inside. "I found it on the floor, next to the kitchen door. If Needles really was here, and he dropped it, it's worth checking out," Jorge said, still suspicious of Hans' story.

"What does *sueños* mean?" the houseboy asked.

"Dreams." Jorge slid the matchbox shut and leaned through the driver side of Nate's car. "I remember seeing this place. It's over on Olympic off La Brea. But I've just never been in. Now's our chance."

"I'll take Hans to the hospital, and pay a visit to Guy Carley while the two of you head to *Sueños* to check it out," Nate offered.

"So much for tracking down Manny Manos." Jorge motioned for Beso to get out of Nate's car.

"Are you sure this is safe?" Beso asked.

"At this point, Beso," Nate replied, "*nothing* is safe. We just have to stay ahead of Mac Needles."

Wishing each other luck, the cousins left for *Sueños* as Nate drove Hans to Cedars-Sinai.

"Now, Nathan, what does that horrible man want with you?" Hans clutched his arm. "I've never seen anyone so fiercely determined before."

Nate filled the houseboy in on the latest discoveries in his manhunt. "From what I know, Needles was a gay film star who just vanished suddenly in the mid-eighties."

"And no one has heard from him since?" Hans finished. "I know the name: Mac Needles. No wonder he looked so familiar. But the look in his eyes was so different!"

"Hans!" Nate exclaimed. "Do you mean to tell me you've met Mac Needles before tonight?"

"Well, yes, in truth I have," Hans said as they turned onto

La Cienega. The cool night had brought a thick, fog-like mist. "Of course it was *years* ago, back when I worked as a dancer at The Bolt. I met a lot of people back then, but I do remember Mac Needles. He was just starting off in porn films. He was hot, and confident. I still remember when he came up to the bar. Everyone wanted him at the time, Nathan. I'll admit, I did, too."

"Hans!" Nate was surprised by the houseboy's confession. "Go on, tell me more!"

"One night I was working and I decided I'd had enough. I mean, he came in all the time, and I know I was a dancer and *I* was the one who was supposed to be doing the teasing. But somehow Mac Needles turned the tables on me. He would eye me and then occupy himself conversing with some other guy. He probably thought I was playing with him, like most dancers. So I decided to let him know I was interested.

"You know how they say that some people reach their peak early? That was truly the summer Mac Needles reached his: the summer of 1986. The frenzy at The Bolt had changed quite a bit that year. Everyone was so worried about HIV. Friends were dying all around us, yet we all still danced and carried on. But now with a suspicion and a caution that never existed before. Even I, Horny Hans, as they called me back then, even I'd begun to exercise a certain restraint I'd never before practiced."

"I remember you telling me it was a sad and terrifying time," Nate said.

"It was. Maybe that's why Mac Needles was so desirable. He looked the way we all wanted to look, Nathan! He was so healthy, so strong, and so masculine, and he just exuded sex appeal! That's why his movies did so well. But, in person, he took things to a whole other level. That's why I *had* to make my move."

"And...?" Nate was eager to hear the rest of the story.

"And..." Hans continued, momentarily forgetting about his sore shoulder. "We'd talked a few times. You know, a casual hello and all that. But one night I came out and asked him if he was interested in me or not." Hans looked out the window, staring off with remembrance. "Actually, I said, 'At some point, you're going to tire of all the other hunks in this bar and take me home.'"

"Hans, what a pick-up line!" Nate laughed. A sprinkling of raindrops began to dot the windshield, and he turned the wipers on, low. "Well? Did it work?"

Hans was somewhat embarrassed by the bravado of his youth. "You know what, Nathan. It did! He even smirked. Then, he gave me his address. He told me to be there at two a.m. when I was done with my dance shift. Of course, I was delighted. Once I finished work, I changed into street clothes, collected my evening cash and drove to this little guest house in the low part of Nichols Canyon. The lights were on and I could hear a record playing as I walked up. Before I could even knock on the door, Mac opened it, a glass of champagne in hand. He beamed, his smile so inviting I suddenly felt myself growing shy. As I walked in, he stepped to the side, and I realized we weren't alone. There, on a beige leather sofa, in cut-off jeans and nothing else, was another guy. He was young and blond, probably my age. I could tell by the interaction between him and Mac they already knew each other well."

"He brought you there for a three-way?" Nate asked. The rain fell harder as they drove, traffic coming to a slow halt, as the drops pounded the hoods of the cars.

"Not exactly!" Hans continued. "When I first walked in, the other guy stared at me, I mean he looked at me, hard. I couldn't tell if he was jealous or disappointed as I was, that he wasn't going to have Mac Needles all to himself. Then, to break silence, Mac asked the other guy, 'Well? What do you think?' The guy kept his gaze on me, and finally lifted himself off the couch, glass of champagne in tow, and just walked around me, examining me, silent until he asked me to take off my shirt.

"Still not knowing what was going on, I sat still, but I *was* growing apprehensive about the situation. I was plenty popular,

Nathan, you know. I hardly needed some boy in cut-offs to decide whether I was okay or not.

"Then Mac started talking. He explained that they were working on a movie together. The other guy, an up and comer named Chase Hastings, and Mac were starting their own production company. There was a dreamlike quality to Mac's voice as he began to tell me about this movie they were working on. But before he could say too much, Chase shushed him and set the champagne down, and looked at me seriously with his crystal blue eyes. 'Have you ever considered a career in porn?' he asked."

"Wow," Nate said, "that's direct. Hans, you never told me you..."

"Quiet, Nathan. Well, this Chase guy was handsome in a boyish way. But he also seemed to be the one in control of the audition. My audition, it turned out. It was evident Mac wanted Chase to be happy with his latest 'find.' When I told him I hadn't considered film before, Mac assured me that their new company wasn't going to produce your typical porn."

"No, it was Desert Heat," Nate said.

"That's exactly the name they used!" Hans exclaimed. "Desert Heat Productions! Mac said that their company would break the barriers between porn and mainstream film. He seemed genuinely sincere and really excited about it."

"So what did you say, Hans?" Nate asked. Had the aging houseboy once had a real stab at being a big porn star?

"Well, before I could give an answer, the phone rang and Mac said he had to leave: it was another potential costar for their new movie. He said he'd be back in a bit, and so my hopes of having a fling with him all went out the window. Ah well. But, at this, Chase relaxed a bit, and for the first time smiled at me. As he heard Mac's car leave the driveway, he said, 'Finally. It's just the two of us!'"

"No! Chase was interested in *you*?"

"From what I understand, Chase was always interested in a

good time. As soon as the car was in the distance, he opened a small drawer in the coffee table and took out a mirrored plate and a bag of coke. 'You'll have to forgive me for not offering sooner,' he explained, 'but Mac frowns upon anything that's illegally mood altering.'"

The houseboy turned uncomfortably toward the young man he had taken such a strong role in rearing. "Now, you have to understand, Nathan, this was a different place and a different time. The wholesome and healthy Hans you know and love, well, let's just say, at the time none of us ever refused *any* kind of 'mood-altering' offer."

"Understood," Nate turned into the hospital's emergency ward parking area. "And, for the record, Hans, the only wholesome and healthy thing about you is your cooking!" The two laughed as they exited the car. Nate made a note that Hans' bleeding had come to a stop. They entered the emergency waiting room, checked Hans in, and then sat down until he was called.

"So that was that!" Hans continued. "We did some blow. We chatted at length. We even toyed around a bit, just to check out our chemistry."

"And…"

"Chase Hastings was very hot, and very seductive. We played around at least an hour, and we did just about everything. I definitely understood Mac's attraction to him, jealous as I may have been of that attraction. He was like a chameleon. Every minute, fulfilling some fantasy I'd had. At the same time, I'd like to think that I was doing the same for him."

"So Chase Hastings had the ability to make his partners believe that they were fulfilling his fantasies." Nate tried to get through the aged houseboy's perhaps selective memory.

Hans ignored the dig and instead sat up proudly. "Let me just say, when all was over, I had the part in the movie!"

"No! You didn't!" Nate exclaimed. "So…then…"

"So I went home. The following morning, the 'script,' and keep in mind it wasn't that much of a script, arrived via messenger and I was scheduled to be at their studio that coming Sunday at two p.m."

Hans sighed, lost in the memory of another time. "I went to the studio that day, and that's when I heard the news. Chase Hastings had died early that very morning!"

"You mean to tell me the movie you were supposed to costar in was *Magic Afternoon*?" Nate asked.

"That's right," Hans reapplied his ice pack. "There had been a car accident. From what I knew of Chase, and from what I heard from people at The Bolt later, that boy sure liked to have a good time. He was with the Barrington twins, who I later found out were also slated to be in *Magic Afternoon*. He was driving his new Chrysler LeBaron convertible down San Vicente Boulevard. Somehow, Chase lost control of the car, skidded over the median into oncoming traffic, and collided with a truck. The Barrington twins and Chase died instantly."

"I read a bio of Chase on the Internet. But it never said how he died."

"Keeping track of who lived and died during those years is virtually impossible. As hot as he and Mac Needles were, Chase Hastings was just one in a billion as far as the rest of the world was concerned. People were dying just as suddenly as Chase Hastings, not from reckless driving, but from AIDS. There was a point where every week I'd find that not just one, but several friends had passed! Needless to say, the party atmosphere at The Bolt began to change…significantly. The bar got emptier. I decided I had to find other work."

"A career in the adult-entertainment field probably wouldn't have been a wise option at that time," Nate reasoned.

"Not only that, Nathan. What Mac and Chase told me about their new production company, and about *Magic Afternoon* in particular, was that the movie would break all remaining barriers. I wanted to be a part of it because I knew it was going to be different. They said it would have a plot, that there would be layers to the characters we'd be playing. It sounded so exciting!

There wasn't much media exposure for gays then. Mac, and I want to say Chase, too, believed that they were going to help bridge that gap.

"At that point, however, in addition to the tragic events we all were dealing with, one shining light for many of us was—and I know this may sound crazy, but it's true—was the advent of the VCR. I could record all my favorite shows while dancing at The Bolt—never missed an episode of *Dynasty* or *Dallas* during all my stripping days—but the VCR also changed the porn industry, too. Before that, if you wanted to watch porn, you had to go and sit through the whole film at the Tomkat Theatre: sticky floor, creaky old theatre seats, and all! But after the VCR, you could just swing by the video store and fast-forward to your favorite part."

"So the concept that Mac Needles had might not have worked after all?"

"Exactly! The ability to fast-forward made us all a little cynical. Who wanted to see characterization in a porn when what you really wanted to see was the money shot?"

"That makes sense," Nate said. But the discovery of Hans' involvement, exciting and coincidental as it was, brought a sobering air to this manhunt. Before Nate could ask more questions about Hans' mysterious past with Mac and Chase, a nurse called his name.

Once Nate had walked the houseboy into the examining room, he excused himself and stopped by the gift shop to purchase a large bouquet of flowers for his other patient, Guy Carley.

After getting the fluffer's room number from the information counter, he boarded the elevator, his mind still lost in thought. Just as the doors were about to close, a doctor, clad in scrubs complete with face mask, made his way into the elevator. Seeing that Nate had already requested the eleventh floor, he leaned against the wall as the doors slid shut.

The discovery of Mac's relationship with Chase, and Hans' explanation of what *Magic Afternoon* could have been, left Nate consumed in thought. No wonder Mac Needles lost it. Despite Nate's newfound empathy for the former porn king, he reminded himself that didn't excuse using an innocent man like Myles Long in some senseless snuff film!

As the arrival of the eleventh floor chimed, the elevator ground to a jarring halt. Snapping out of his thoughts, Nate realized the doctor on board had opened the elevator panel and commanded the stop himself!

"What are you doing?" Nate asked as the doctor turned slowly toward him, his dark eyes wild with rage. Before Nate could contemplate his next move, the lights clicked off, leaving him in darkness.

"After all those viewings of the elevator scene in *The Straight Shooter*, I thought you'd enjoy an extended ride up this particular shaft," the assailant hissed, his muscular frame pushing Nate against the control panel.

"Who are you?"

"All this investigating on your manhunt, and you still haven't figured that out?" The man traced a finger slowly down Nate's face, erupting a sweat throughout his entire body.

"Why, you must be Mac Needles." Nate's rapid breath cut every word short.

"That sounded more like a question than the sort of answer I'd expect from you. Perhaps it's time to drop this manhunt and move on to other things." His warm body moved so close to Nate's, he could barely squirm. Through the thin cotton of the scrubs, Nate could feel the man stiffen against his thigh.

"I'll stop investigating when I've found my man," Nate said as his rebellious body grew warmer to every touch of the assailant, responding in ways he wasn't prepared for. As the large cock pushed up against Nate, he could feel his own cock harden in response. Despite his mission, there was no resisting the heat Nate felt at that moment. Was this the same feeling Guy's friend had that Christmas? Roger told Guy he felt as if Mac was trying to break him, make him succumb to him in ways he wasn't prepared for. Was Mac now casting the same spell upon Nate? His present persistence had a similar hypnotic effect, an uncompromising force that made Nate feel he was left no option but to give in.

Sensing this moment of weakness, the man grabbed his crotch tightly, his breath heavy against Nate's face.

"How about *I* say when you're finished, Firecrotch? Let's say you stop when, and only when, I'm satisfied." Still pushing Nate against the wall, Mac reached behind and pulled at the waist of the redhead's pants, his hand cupping Nate's left buttock with a possessive squeeze.

"I'll stop once Myles Long is safely home!" Nate's logic took control of the overheated situation. His hand felt around behind his back, exploring the buttons on the control panel, stopping at a large, bulbous switch. As the man closed in on him, he pressed his body against the button. A shrieking alarm filled the small cabin!

Jerking back in panic, the man pushed Nate down to the ground and fumbled frantically with the panel. The doors of the elevator sprang open. Quickly, the man leapt out and tore down the hall. As Nate ran out behind him, he found that the man had vanished, but heard the click of a heavy door. The stairway! Flying down floor by floor, he made his way to the last landing and opened the door. The main lobby was empty.

Exhausted, Nate rested at the bottom stair. He saw that the face mask and scrubs the attacker had worn were now crumpled in the corner of the stairwell.

Deciding against another elevator ride, Nate caught his breath and opted to take the stairs back up. He headed down the long, sterile hallway to room 1124. As he neared the door, the clean hospital smell was polluted by a strong stench. Cigar smoke? Nate wondered. Indeed it was, he realized, as he opened the door and saw a gray cloud escape.

"Guy?" Nate said in recognition of the smell. Didn't the

old fluffer know there was no smoking in the hospital? To his surprise, a tall, gray-haired, heavyset woman in white turned around and gasped at being discovered.

"Dear me," she hid the cigar behind her wide frame. "Don't report me to the head nurse!"

"I just recognized the smell and thought it was Guy Carley's room. I apologize."

"This *is* his room," she replied, relaxing and taking another puff off the cigar. "Or, I should say, it *was* his room."

"I see." Nate set the flowers on a table and noticed the bed had been made up and the room prepped for a new patient. A dreadful possibility dawned on Nate, one he wasn't even willing to consider aloud. "Has he moved to another room?"

"Guy?" she snickered. "No! I'm afraid your boy's hit the road! Soon as he got me to take the I.V. out, that boy hightailed it outta here like you wouldn't believe."

"So he's alive," Nate said, relieved. "I'm a friend and wanted to check on him."

"You're lucky your friend *is* alive. Someone did real damage on that fella. I'd sting the brute and give him a good ass-whupping, too, if I could." She paused, regained control, and stubbed the cigar out on a medical supply tray. "Where's my manners? I'm Nurse Nell. Pleasure to meet you."

"And to meet you, Nell, I'm—" Nate extended his hand to the friendly, if weathered, nurse. She grabbed it, winking at him from behind smudged glasses.

"No introduction necessary. I know who you are, fella! You're Rhett Rosebud."

"How did you know that…" Nate was relieved that his cover remained in place.

"How do you think I got these cigars in the first place? Been talking to that feisty Cooter since he checked in. Once I heard his story, I helped that sweet man escape before he had yet another attempt made on his life. He told me all about his day. Enough to make you wanna leave and start all over again." She examined the cigar ashes and, satisfied the embers were out, tossed it into a waste bin. "Which is exactly what he went to do. I don't reckon you'll see Guy Carley anytime soon. He was terrified for his life. Said he almost got killed by a ghost from his past. A ghost from his past? Just like in a Judith Krantz novel!"

"I'm just glad he's all right," Nate said, relieved.

"I suspect he's high in the sky, flying to some exotic island to hide out. He told me you might be by to check on him. So it *is* you, Rhett Rosebud?"

"Guy and I met earlier today."

"Forgive me for not being familiar with your 'work,' though I guess you don't really appeal to my demographic. I've been a Nielsen family, but I don't think what you do for a living actually ever airs on public television!" The nurse laughed at her own joke, rummaging through paperwork. "Well. Time to make my rounds."

"Listen, Nurse Nell, did Guy tell you where he was going?"

"He wouldn't even tell me in what time zone it was! But I will say this, you li'l firecracker, you made *quite* an impression on him, 'cause he gave me all these for two reasons." She grabbed the box of cigars with excitement.

"One reason being that I helped expedite his check-out." She dug midway through her stack of paperwork, at which point she produced a letter-sized envelope. "The second reason being that I make sure you, Rhett Rosebud, get this here letter."

PART THREE: ANA BENDER

SIGUE TUS SUEÑOS

I'm so fucking wet," Beso squealed as he and Jorge escaped from the pounding rain into the bar.

"Careful, Beso! You might give everyone the wrong idea!" Jorge laughed as he stood with his cousin at the entrance to *Sueños*. Mid-eighties Hi-NRG dance music played in the all-but-deserted room. To their left, a long bar in the dim shadows was almost an afterthought, compared to the well-lit stage in the center. Metal folding chairs surrounded the stage, all flipped open. But by this point of the night, perhaps as a result of the rainstorm, only a few men sat in the chairs, all three of them Latinos, with flannel shirts tucked into jeans. In response to the cousins' dramatic arrival, the men pulled their cowboy hats lower, so only their thick bristled mustaches were visible.

"What kind of place is this?" Beso stage-whispered. "Oh no! Toto, I have a feeling we're not in West Hollywood anymore!"

Before Jorge could respond, the music switched to syncopated drumbeats and a synthesizer ignited the room, and a black drag queen with a long, spiked Mohawk jumped onstage. "She's—on to—you!" sang the backup singers, punctuating the beat. The queen—her tall and manly build accentuated by a glittering black blazer with pancake-sized shoulder pads—slid up and down the stage, "Been tellin' lies, sweet alibis," she mouthed, sliding offstage and gliding past the empty chairs of the audience. "You better run, boy! She's got your game."

She managed to get a dollar bill stuffed into her bustier by each man and eyed the new arrivals with interest, then began dancing and gyrating to the back of the room. The well-rehearsed spotlight struggled to keep up with her impromptu moves. "She's onto you. What can I do? The lies we told, boy. My love's to blame!" Up close, the queen was large and intimidating. Yellow and gold eye shadow ended abruptly with dark, thick streaks of electric blue eye liner that made her eyes look calculating. She stopped lip-synching momentarily and then smiled, large crooked teeth all but destroying the glam image she barely possessed.

"Hi, boys," she said to Beso and Jorge. "Come stay awhile." She waved her long, painted hand at the dark bar, where a well-muscled figure leaned atop the counter.

"We gotta be careful," she continued mouthing the lyrics, returning to the original, more traditional audience, of *Sueños*, "Now that she knows, she's on your tail wherever you go."

"This place *es muy extraño*, Jorge," Beso said.

"You can say that *otra vez*," Jorge agreed. "Now I *really* need a drink!"

"Just don't drink the water," Beso cautioned.

"Beso, I know it might seem like it, but we're not *really* in Mexico!" Putting on a false front of confidence, Jorge sat at a bar stool and pulled one next to him out for Beso. Hesitantly, his cousin joined him.

"Hey, guys." The bartender frisbeed two cardboard drink coasters at the newcomers. "What can I get for you?"

Jorge's jaw dropped in recognition. "I...uh..." he stammered.

"What my cousin *means* to say," Beso interrupted, "is we'd like two Coronas and two shots of your finest tequila."

The bartender smiled, flashing a silver-capped tooth, and then winked at Jorge before walking to the cooler to retrieve beer.

Beso nudged Jorge in his side, laughing because, for once,

the sassy Latin playboy was at a loss for words. "What's the matter, *Jorgito*? Hot bartender got your tongue?"

"Oh," Jorge stammered, "*en mis sueños!* Beso, do you know who that *is*?"

"I don't care if he's Enrique Iglesias, as long as I get my drink on and stay out of the rain."

"That's Manny Manos! Talk about killing two *pájaros* with one stone. This is perfect!" He sat back comfortably as the bartender produced the beer then poured a generous portion of tequila into each shot glass.

"Cheers," he said. "Can I get you boys anything else?"

"An autograph, perhaps," Jorge said, perkily. "Forgive me if I'm wrong. But aren't you Manny Manos?"

The bartender looked bashfully at the floor a moment, before his caramel eyes met Jorge's. "The one and only!"

Though Jorge couldn't relate to Nate's attraction to Myles Long in *The Straight Shooter*, a few costars—first Buck Steers, then, later on in the film, Manny Manos were exactly up his alley. The scene in the film with Manny Manos was Jorge's favorite.

It is approaching midafternoon, and the summer heat is beginning to take its toll on pedestrians as they work up a sweat hurrying to and from home and work. Shots of city life, hot men trying to stay cool, and bumper-to-bumper traffic fill the beginning of the scene. The camera zooms tight on a black Cadillac Escalade pulling into the infamous Santa Palm Car Wash. Myles Long maneuvers his SUV in, rolling down the window and letting the car-wash attendant know that he wants "The Works." He comes face-to-face with Manny Manos. Instantly, Myles Long's mysterious mind-reading ability shifts into gear as he hears Manny's less-than-pure thoughts: "I'd love him to give *me* The Works," the car-wash attendant thinks loudly.

Smirking at the young attendant's inner desire made manifest, Myles nods for Manny to get into the passenger seat. "Need help soaping up?" the attendant offers as Long proceeds into the automatic wash. Water and steam cover every window of the Escalade and they find themselves locked in a heated make-out session. Soon, Manny finds himself hungrily sucking Myles as the mind-reader lets his hand trail down the attendant's well-bleached, well-oiled bum! During the rinse cycle, Myles enters Manny's ass and gives it a good pumping as the SUV goes through similar motions, building up to the Hot Wax climax— during which both studs shoot all over each other while outside suds go flying everywhere.

"That scene was far too short, in my opinion," Jorge raved to the moonlighting porn star. "I think you were robbed of precious screen time!"

"*Gracias.*" Manny blushed as he licked his lips. "I've only done films like that a few times. When it's kinda slow here. Or when my family needs the money. But I enjoy playing those parts."

"*Sí.*" Beso cackled, the tequila making him extra bitchy. "I can only imagine."

"Actually," Jorge said, "we came here because of your costar, Myles Long."

"Really?" Manny lit up, "He wants to do it again? Fuck, man, I enjoyed it for sure, you know."

"Oh, I'm sure he'd *love* to do it again," Jorge enthused, a bit vicariously. "But we're here because Myles is missing! A friend was with him a few days ago when two men jumped out of a van and abducted Myles."

"You serious, *hombre*?"

"Es-tremely. We think one of the men involved recently died. We have reason to believe the other had contact with Myles, during the filming of *The Straight Shooter*. Maybe you've seen him?"

"And," Beso added, finishing a second shot that Manny bought for his new fans, "we also have reason to believe the man we're looking for was here at *Sueños* recently."

"No way, man," Manny said, then: "Well, shit! What'd he look like?"

"That's the problem, we only have one picture of him," Jorge motioned for Beso to dig through his book bag. "We got it off the Internet and it's from twenty years ago. But we hope despite its vintage you'll still be able to recognize him."

Manny held the photo under a small reading light near the cash register. "*Sí*, I know this dude. Name is Mac?"

"Mac Needles," Beso responded enthusiastically. "So! You've met him."

Manny leaned against the bar. "Oh yeah! He started coming here all the time, about three months ago. He'd seen me in the movie, too. So we got along real good. Not many dudes who come in want to talk to me, you know? Most of them want to see the show."

"Did he ever say anything about Myles Long?" Jorge tried to remain calm despite his excitement in such a great lead.

"Yeah, man. That's *all* he could talk about. He pretended to act all casual about it and shit. But he was practically coming in his pants to get hold of Myles. Don't get me wrong, Myles is hot, but this dude was *really* into him. So, I hooked them up to meet. Myles was on summer break. I told him he should come and check out *Sueños*, and see another side of L.A. life, you know?"

"How did that meeting go?" Beso asked.

"They *seemed* to hit it off. I mean, I set it up that Mac was just a bar regular. I didn't want to scare my little buddy away." Manny laughed, again flashing his silver-capped front tooth. "All I know is, they chatted and agreed to meet for dinner a few nights later. I don't know much else after that. But from what Mac said when he came in tonight, the two became good pals."

"Mac Needles was *here tonight*?" Jorge locked eyes with Beso, both of them realizing the lost matchbook was a bigger clue than either had bargained for.

"He pops in now and again. I hadn't seen him for a few weeks, but he said he and Myles were staying in touch and getting along, *cómo se dice*, famously."

Jorge leaned forward. "Did Mac say where he lives, or anything along that line?"

Manny shifted nervously as he rubbed his arm, his eyes suddenly alive. "So, you think this fool kidnapped Myles? Shit, he didn't seem like that kind of dude."

"We have good reason to believe 'this fool' is dangerous, Manny!" Beso warned, eyeing the bartender's muscular arms. "Though it looks as if you would have no problem defending yourself, we just thought you *should* know."

"Thanks for the warning," Manny said, semi-stunned by the news.

Jorge finished the Corona and jotted his phone number down on the coaster. "If anything else comes up, Manny, give us a call. Anything at all," and then he added, "We're trying everything we can to save Myles Long."

"We think his life is in danger. We've had a few run-ins with Mac, and aside from being extremely well-endowed, he's tons of trouble," Beso added.

"I definitely will," Manny agreed, growing silent as he digested the bad news.

"You can always call this number, even if you don't have any leads. Maybe if you need someone to talk to," Jorge added hopefully.

Manny Manos beamed his trademark, silver-toothed, porn-film smile as he tucked the beer-dampened coaster into a jeans pocket. "We can chat, dude. But when I'm off camera I prefer a different type. No offense."

"None taken," Jorge said unconvincingly.

"Now if you were a light-skinned redhead—that would be a different story. I really like dudes with *el pelo rojo*. You know? And freckles? Don't even get me started." Manny licked his lips.

"Well, we have a friend you'd love to meet," Beso said, even as Jorge smacked his arm.

"But we simply must be going." Jorge threw some cash on the bar and motioned for Beso to get up.

"Don't leave so soon," a voice pled from behind. Turning, they saw the large diva who'd performed earlier. She was holding an oversized, half-filled martini glass aloft as she tilted toward the bar. Beso and Jorge looked at her uncomfortably, then Beso jumped in recognition.

"Wait one minute! I know who you are. Aren't you Ana Bender?"

"I am—usually." The heavyset queen winked a falsely eyelashed eye at them. "However, here at *Sueños*…"

"She's Ana *Gaucho*," Manny finished, handing the diva a double vodka martini.

"And tonight, I'm not getting on *any* of those three *gauchos*," she said, dismissing them as she saddled up to the bar. "Don't get me wrong." She took a long sip of her cocktail. "Just because I'm not Ana Bender tonight doesn't mean I can't *go* on a bender!"

The cousins laughed with her as she took another gulp of her giant martini. "Do say, boys, that you'll stay and have one more drink with lonely little me? Dear Man-u-el here and I… well, we only have so much to discuss that we haven't *already* discussed." She set down her glass and opened a compact mirror, checking out her gold eye shadow and touching up slightly with a brush. "I'm sure you can only imagine how the two of us have been guilty of getting bored with one another. Haven't we, Man-u-el?"

"'Fraid that is so, Ana," Manny agreed.

"If Manuel hears one more story of how I scored my latest wig, or how I wish the eighties had never ended, he may spike my streaming supply of cocktails with arsenic!" She patted the seats the two had occupied. "Let me get you two one more drinkee before you venture out into that bone-chilling rain!"

The cousins looked at each other before settling back onto

their bar stools. Beso flopped his book bag back onto the bartop. "I, for one, have *never* refused a nightcap."

"Then it's done!" Ana Bender commanded. "Manny, three double martinis, and get some of those Fritos while you're at it. So," she turned to the cousins, "whatever brings you boys out on a night like tonight?"

"Just exploring." Jorge countered, "What brings *you* out on a night like tonight?"

"Girl's gotta pay the rent," Ana stated with an air of the obvious as she leaned back in her chair. "I'm guessing you boys recognized me from The Tavern. That's where I usually am. But my boss there's such a tight bitch I can't get an extra nickel out of her."

"Anitra Tucci?" Beso asked, reaching for the bowl of Fritos.

Ana stopped, surprised. "Wow! You boys really know the Who's Ho of WeHo." Ana laughed at her witticism. "I *am* impressed. Now, don't go calling the tabloids on account of my sassy statements. Anitra and I go *way back*. But that girl didn't get to where she's at today by giving handouts."

"You've mean you've known each other for a long time?" Jorge asked.

"We knew each other *way back when*. I know what you're thinking, what is a high-powered female executive doing, hanging out with a drunken old queen like me?" Ana assumed, laughing at herself. "It *is* getting warm in here!" She reached into her purse for a large, patterned fan. "My heavens!"

"You are such a hoot, Ana!" Beso exclaimed. "Tell us more!"

"I can tell you everything you need to know about this one," Manny said as he set down the three martinis. "You might know her as just that drag queen hosting the shows at The Tavern, but Ana Bender *née* Gaucho has been around a whole lot longer than that."

"All...too...true," Ana confessed humbly. "Longer than I care to admit. Thankfully, Botox and my thick, dark skin ward age off to the best of their ability."

"Emphasis on the best of their ability." Manny laughed. "Well, she's not gonna brag, but Ana used to go by a different name in the eighties." His tale was interrupted by the shrill ring of a phone by the cash register.

"Man-u-el! That was just between us," she said coyly as the bartender went to answer the phone. "But it's true." Ana turned to the cousins, visibly pleased that Manny had created an entrée to her life story. "Still, you boys are *much too young* to remember that far back. Why, I'm sure you were still in diapers in those days...when I used to go by the name of Jen Bender. As in Gender-Bender."

"Like Boy George?" Jorge asked.

"Or his bitchy nemesis, Marilyn!" Beso replied, recalling a recent lesson from his Gay Pop Culture primer. "Don't think I don't know a bit about the eighties myself, Ana!"

"I can see that," Ana said with a quick wave of her fan.

Manny returned to the group. "Either of you drive a blue Mini Cooper?"

"That's me," Jorge said, setting his glass down.

"One of the gauchos called from the parking lot. You left your lights on."

"Dios mío!" the buff Latino cried. "I'll be right back."

Ana watched Jorge leave and returned her attention to Beso. "Marilyn! I forgot all about her. Well, when those stars were hot, we *all* were in vogue. Everyone in that day, especially all of the New Romance bands of that era, was dying to have Yours Truly in their videos."

As if on cue, Manny presented a photo album of the drag queen's head shots. The now full-figured queen appeared young and feline in the photos, her lips always in a trademark pout that also served to cover up her messed-up grill.

"You look so beautiful," Beso enthused. "I think I saw you in that *His Name is Charlie* video I saw at Retro Night."

"You are one sharp cookie!" Ana said brightly. "That's how Anitra and I know each other. When Gender-Benders were the rage, Jen Bender got invited *everywhere*! Needless to say, I used almost every invitation I got as a press junket. Free publicity? Hello! I was getting invited to all the clubs on the Sunset Strip, and though Anitra Tucci is very together these days, that girl used to *love* to party. She was on the arm of a new guy every weekend. She'd smile like a toothpaste ad! And she could really tie one on."

"Here's to tying one on," Manny produced another round of martinis.

"She was a bad girl, that Anitra. But…we loved her," Ana seemed lost in thought as she finished off the new drink in one greedy gulp.

Beso studied the drag queen, who was staring off into space, the effects of the rapid imbibing definitely catching up. "We all have to go through our naughty phase," the stocky cousin supplied. "Why, even *I've* been known to—"

"Naughty?" Ana snapped, glaring at Beso angrily, her gracious and flamboyant demeanor suddenly turning dark, *"Naughty?"* She flagged Manny down, pushing her freshly emptied glass forward.

"I'm sorry, Ana," Beso was surprised by her sudden mood swing. "I didn't mean to offend you."

The queen continued to stare straight ahead at the bar, shoving handfuls of Fritos into her mouth, gnashing the curled chips in fury. All crunching aside, a deafening silence fell as they waited for Ana's fourth martini to arrive. Upon its delivery, she took a long sip before turning to Beso, eyes bleary with the effect of vodka, her glossy lips speckled with Frito crumbs. "If you only knew how *naughty* that bitch has been!"

❖

The rain slowed to a drizzle as Jorge stumbled down the dark alleyway to the parking lot. His head spinning from the dangerous mix of beer, vodka, tequila, and the protein shake he'd enjoyed earlier, he eyed the closed-up taco truck parked along the brick wall of the club. What I'd do for a *torta*!, he thought sadly, turning past the chain link fence into the lot. Glistening from the fresh rain, his blue Mini Cooper sat alone in the lot, the headlights off.

"What the..." he said aloud, sliding into the car and turning it on to ensure the battery still worked. Satisfied after clicking the headlights on and then off again, he turned the car off, set the alarm, and made his way back down the alleyway. He shivered and clenched his teeth as the cold droplets grew heavier and faster on his bare arms. A loud thunder clap shook the narrow road, causing Jorge to grab the brick wall to steady himself. His pulse quickened and he broke into a run, each splashing step echoing against the close walls of the alley.

The thunder started again, followed by the squeal of tires as the lights of the taco truck clicked on! Backing away, Jorge shielded his gaze from the headlights and attempted to make out the driver in the cab. Behind the wheel, the silhouette of a man in a large cowboy hat loomed before him.

It was one of the gauchos!

The horn of the rumbling truck filled the alley with a cacophonous melody: *La cucaracha, la cucaracha*. Turning back to the parking lot, Jorge raced away from the truck, its engine revving as it charged right at him.

Slipping on the wet pavement, he managed to remain just inches ahead of the front bumper. As he came upon the chain link fence, the truck gave him mere seconds to scale the fence before it crashed into the exact place where he had just stood!

Hanging from above the truck, he attempted to catch his breath and look down into the window of the cab, but the driver's hat was pulled down so low he could only see that his big fake mustache was coming undone on the left side, revealing a pair of full lips. Grabbing the microphone in the truck, the driver clicked the P.A. system, interrupting the musical horn with a loud squeal.

"What do you want?" Jorge asked desperately.

The man remained silent, his heavy breathing echoing from the loudspeaker.

"*Basta!* I've had enough of this!" Trembling, Jorge lowered himself to get a better view of the man. Sensing this, the driver flipped down the visor, slammed the taco truck into reverse, and screeched down to the opening of the alleyway, backing onto the street and tearing off into the night.

MEMOIRS OF A FLUFFER

Dear Rhett,

By the time you read this I'll be somewhere far away. Hopefully safe from what I encountered earlier today. I'm sure you're wondering why you, of all people, are receiving a letter from me, considering we only just met. But I have to tell you it has more to do with what we discussed prior to my attack than anything else. You see, while you were in the studio, getting ready for your scene with Gino Rantelli, I came face-to-face with the man we had been discussing, Mac Needles himself! Only he wasn't the same Mac I knew from long ago. Something was different, something was missing, I want to say. He was still as physically attractive as ever, and he had the same steely look that drove his fans wild. But something about that look had turned cold and empty; the look in his eyes was now vacant. It almost seemed there was no life in his face.

Somehow, Mac had overheard us talking, because he warned me to keep my mouth shut. That's the last thing I remember. Then I woke up in this hospital room. My throat was still sore from him attempting to strangle me!

What was he trying to keep me from telling you? I

wonder. What did I say that should have been subjected to secrecy? I've been lying here in this hospital room trying to make sense of it all, why he was so desperate about me keeping my silly tales to myself.

Nothing registered until I was watching the local news. A story showed Anitra Tucci at The Tavern, appealing to the public in her search for missing porn star, Myles Long. You've probably figured out by now, I'm not one for mainstream porn. I don't think I've sat through a Vanilla Flick in a good twenty years, but when I saw that close-up picture of Myles Long on the TV screen, a few things began to make sense.

I told you Mac Needles was only with Chapped Hide a brief time, a time of tension and unpredictability. All of us were trying to adapt our studios to the surging demand for home video sales. The way we had made movies had to change to a faster, less expensive, more streamlined "means of production," so we could make multiple releases. It was exciting and challenging. But Mac wanted nothing to do with it. He hated anything having to do with videotape. At one point, during the "Death Row Orgy" release party, where Mac headlined as a correctional officer, he went up to the video monitor, ejected the tape, and unraveled it, hitting the producer over the head with the cassette!

It was clear our relationship with Needles couldn't continue. I really felt for the guy: his previous production company folded due to the sudden death of his partner, Chase Hastings. Being subjected to the roles at another production house was more than he could take. I later found out that wasn't the only thing upsetting Mac.

The story I didn't tell you, but should have, was more personal in nature. You see, when I saw Myles Long's photo on the hospital television, his resemblance to Chase Hastings was undeniable. The same curly blond hair, same seductive smile, same boyish ruggedness of Chase. What Mac wanted to keep me from telling you, even to the point of killing me, is that I know he had to be responsible for the abduction.

I had already told you about my friend Roger, whose looks alone were similar to Chase's, even though somewhat of a stretch. What I didn't tell you was what happened the day after Mac was fired from Chapped Hide. I was the only one in the studio who seemed able to empathize with Mac, and I was assigned the dubious task of delivering his final check. I made my way to Mac's place, a tiny guest house in Nichols Canyon, but at the entrance, I noticed the door slightly open. I stepped in, slowly walked through the living room, made my way through many empty cartons of Chinese take-out, old beer cans, and dirty clothes scattered all about. I called Mac's name, but heard no response. Initially, I was convinced his house had been robbed and ransacked. But as I moved past the kitchen, I realized I'd entered the den of someone in deep depression. The sink and countertop overflowed with dirty china, three garbage cans stood filled to the brim. The stench of rotting garbage was overwhelming, but then I began to breathe in a more prevalent odor—burning plastic. From the kitchen, I made out a bright light at the end of the hall, the smell stronger as I approached. Pushing the door open, I was in Mac's bedroom and there he was, naked on the bed, a TV atop his dresser showing a clip of him and Hastings having sex, stacks of photo albums, film loops, and clothing burning in a big pile in the center of the room.

"What are you doing?" I asked as smoke filled the room. I coughed, trying to pull him off the bed. He sat there, transfixed by the movie scene, embroiled in his own self-created hell, eyes red from the smoke, still staring at the television.

The guest house now engulfed in flames, the smoke detector began ringing. I grabbed Mac by his underarms and attempted to get him out of the room. He was unresponsive, limp and heavier by the minute, as though determined to stay in the inferno. To this day I don't know how I managed to get him out. We made it outdoors, and I took a denim jacket from my car and covered him with it. I remember saying, "Are you crazy? This ain't worth it!" But as he lay on the lawn, across the driveway from the burning house, he just stared up at the sky.

Eventually, fire trucks arrived, and they moved us down the road and worked to control the blaze. The police arrived and questioned me, but they seemed to assume that Needles was guilty. "This is our third call at this address in a week," one of the cops muttered as they cuffed him and shoved him into the squad car. "Looks like he lost it, because this time he's succeeded!"

That was the last I saw of Mac for some time. I heard, months later, he was released from a mental ward and recovering. But I knew his life would never be the same. Two years after the fire, I tracked him down. He was living in a small apartment in Simi Valley and working at a gas station. When I came in the gas station, he smiled the same warm smile he'd had back in his Desert Heat days. He told me he was off at four that afternoon and we agreed to meet for a beer.

"I don't think any of us knew," I told him, "how much you loved Chase Hastings."

He sipped his beer and said, "When you found me in the guest house, I'd decided I couldn't stand missing him another minute. I took everything that reminded me of him, every picture, every piece of clothing, every movie he'd made, I threw it into that pile and set it afire. I didn't care if I died, I just wanted it to go away!"

We talked, and it seemed like he'd come to some sort of peace, out there in the middle of Nowheresville, at a gas station, of all places!

I didn't think of him again until the following year. I was driving back from a trip up north and decided to stop at that same gas station, to see if Mac was still working there. There was a kid in his place, a pimple-faced, sixteen-year-old boy with dirty brown hair in need of a good cut. When I asked him about Mac, he stared at me blankly, shrugged and said he didn't know. A short, stocky, woman behind the counter, came out and asked to see me outside. She said Mac had been there 'til three months ago, when a group of gay guys stopped in the gas station and recognized him. "They were clawing at him like you wouldn't believe!" she said.

"When more guys began coming around for him, the owner of the gas station asked Mac to leave." In the midst of all these visits by fans, one guy told Mac he had a bootleg copy of "Magic Afternoon" that he'd gotten from a friend. Mac snapped, pushed the guy into a rack of candy bars, and demanded the video. Before he could respond, Mac started hitting him! The other shoppers in the gas station had to hold him back. The very mention of "Magic Afternoon" had sent him into a tailspin!

I wanted to find him, help him get through this bad time. I'd never met Chase; I could only imagine how hard such a sudden death must be. Every place I searched turned up nothing that could lead me to Mac's whereabouts. When I heard Roger's tale that Christmas, I made one last attempt to find him. But the Silverlake apartment that Roger directed me to had been emptied out and was up for rent.

Lying here in this room, preparing to escape, none of us know where Mac Needles is. But there's no doubt in my mind he's responsible for Myles Long's disappearance. His resemblance to Chase Hastings is so close, there's no way this can end on a happy note! As I told you before, I still remember how he said to Roger, "Leave while you still can." I can only imagine what he truly meant.

Hasta la Vista

Daddy Guy

MEMBERS ONLY

It was late morning when the investigating trio convened for breakfast at The Tavern to catch each other up on the discoveries of the previous evening.

Sipping heavily on a much-needed Bloody Mary, Beso read Guy's account of Mac's descent into madness. As breakfast arrived, Beso returned the letter to Nate. "This makes total sense!" Beso said between bites of cream cheese and peach-stuffed french toast. "After Chase's death, Mac's heart was so broken that Myles' similarity made him completely nutso!"

"If he loves the guy so much, why would he put him in a snuff film?" Jorge questioned. He leaned back to reveal his most recent purchase: a Tucci tank top proclaiming *Must Be Five Feet or Taller to Enjoy This Ride.*

"Because he wants no memory left of the guy. Even the mention of *Magic Afternoon* drove him insane. It doesn't take much to make this guy snap. So imagine he's driving down the street, and sees a billboard with a guy who looks exactly like the lover he's lost?"

"I guess," Jorge agreed. He was applying slight pressure on his temples with his index fingers, still reeling from his excessive alcohol intake of the previous night.

"Look, there's the video clip Guy wrote about." Nate pointed at the flat-panel TV hung above the bar. In the clip, airing yet again, Tucci made a public plea to find Myles Long.

"With the investments Tucci made in her gay empire, and without the help of her newest and biggest star, Myles Long," a reporter said over the scene, "she now may need a way to keep her overextended company afloat."

Tucci leaned into the interviewer, dabbing her eyes with tissue as the crowd cried, "Find him! Find him! Find him!"

"*Hijos*, we missed all the fun," Beso said as the camera scanned the crowd that stormed The Tavern the night before.

"And, to help make sure my dear friend, Myles Long, is returned to us," Tucci continued in the clip, "I'm giving all you in the audience a gift." Opening a small bag, she lifted out a pale blue tank top with a glittery decal depicting Myles Long and the phrase *Find Him!* in bold print. The determined cries of the crowd rose in response.

"Damn!" Jorge snapped, crossing his arms over his now passé tank top. "I sure didn't get one of those at *Sueños*! All I got was a death threat."

"From a guy in a taco truck!" Beso said between bites. "Tack-ee! This whole manhunt is becoming a bit…multicultural!"

"It's odd the driver didn't do *more* damage." Nate examined a small bruise on his friend's arm. "Once you climbed the gate, I'm surprised he didn't pull a gun."

"He very well could have, but his mustache kept coming undone from his face. That's what happens when you buy a cheap *disfraz*. The closer I got to his window, the more *nervioso* this dude got. He put the truck in reverse and tore out of the alleyway before I could see him up close. It doesn't matter. I might as well *be dead* with this rotten-ass hangover!"

"I, for one, have never eaten so many Fritos in my life." Beso set his fork down and pushed the empty plate away. "That Ana Bender is slimming trouble with a capital T!"

"It sounds like Ana has secrets about Tucci. Her resentment seems to go beyond getting poorly paid for gigs at The Tavern."

"Who knows?" Jorge said in exasperation. "Ana went from pleasant and sweet to mean and nasty, in half a martini."

"Which, given her pace of drinking them, was all of three minutes," Beso added. "I agree with Nate. There's definitely something going on with Bender. She may have even played a role in the whole taco truck debacle. It might be a good idea to see her again, only this time let's *not* drink at her pace."

Nate nodded. "If she has something to say, she's going to say it *after* a few cocktails. You already said Manny Manos talks to her all the time."

"He even had a few stories of his own about her," Beso said. "The real trick will be to keep Ana intoxicated, yet not so much that she passes out."

"You can say that again, cousin." Jorge recalled Ana Bender falling off the bar stool. "If we hadn't caught her, all those trashy little tales of hers could have been history."

"How did she get home?" Nate asked. "Don't tell me you left her there at *Sueños*!"

"We drove her home. You try getting a two hundred fifty pound queen up to the third floor of an apartment building."

"Nice place, though," Beso revealed. "Definitely a queen's digs. Beautiful twenties-style condo in Larchmont Village."

"Wow," Nate said in bewilderment. "So much for being poorly paid by Tucci."

"It was nice, but the lack of an elevator was a major drawback. We both got a good workout hauling that *chica* upstairs!"

"Do you have time to visit her today?" Nate asked. "Just be her good, new friends, checking up on someone who wasn't doing so well last night?"

"Good idea," Beso agreed. "We can bring flowers or candy—"

"Or a bottle of Grey Goose," Jorge added. "I mean, let's face it, they don't call her Ana Bender for nothing." The buff young Latino's cell phone buzzed, signaling a new text message. "Maybe that's her, asking us how we made it home last night." Reviewing the message, he realized it was from his other new friend from the previous evening, Manny Manos.

So pinche horny today. You wanna help?

Jorge promptly texted back, Absolutely.

I have more dirt on Mac Needles also.

Sounds like a meeting that will serve dual purposes.

However, Jorge was in for a rude awakening when he received Manny's reply:

How's this? I'll supply the info on how to find Needles. You supply that foxy redheaded friend of yours! Just thinking about his freckles gets my pinga hard!

Jorge gasped and hesitated, glaring at Nate chatting unawares with Beso. He sighed before texting back:

Deal.

To which Manny replied, Tell your friend to meet me at Vapor Baths at 8 PM. That way, we can take care of both his needs and mine.

Jorge closed his phone and threw it on the table. "For just one night, I wish I had red hair and freckles. Damn you, Nate Dainty!"

Beso laughed heartily. "He's just jealous because Manny Manos has a weakness for redheads. I showed him a picture of you on my cell phone and he practically wet himself."

"Get out!" Nate laughed in disbelief. "Are you serious?"

"We are motherfucking serious!" Jorge said. "So serious he wants to meet you personally at the Vapor Baths." Reluctantly, he revealed the text to the others.

"He has more information!" Nate exclaimed.

"Apparently." Jorge feigned disinterest and covered his bruised ego. "Or he could just be trying to get you into the sack."

"This manhunt of yours certainly is filling your social calendar, Nate!" Beso observed. "And it's also giving me the most severe hangovers of my *vida*. If I miss one more day of school I'll be expelled from my Gay Pop Culture class."

"That makes two of us," Jorge agreed.

The three agreed to part ways. As Beso and Jorge hurried off to class, they also planned a time to visit Ana Bender, to get more information on Anitra Tucci.

Nate waved good-bye to the duo, watching the midmorning crowd dwindle. Sipping his latte, Nate realized that at least half of the men that morning now wore Tucci's latest tank top. Myles Long's face was everywhere. Noting how much the tide of this manhunt had turned in the past day, he decided to visit the woman in question herself. Along the corridor to Tucci's office, he noticed the hustle and bustle he had witnessed last time at the office had slowed to a crawl. "I guess Tucci's workers aren't exactly morning people," the young redhead said to himself as he neared her office door.

At the door, he made out Tucci's voice, the same delivery and tone from previous encounters, but more urgent. Before making his presence known, he stood beside the frosted glass door to eavesdrop.

"I won't be threatened any longer," the producer trilled as Nate made out her silhouette pacing back and forth in the stark office. "You know as well as I do we *both* have secrets. Revealing this would not only be disaster for me, but for you, too."

Nate leaned closer, listening to Tucci pace, her forceful laughs countered with long, exasperated sighs. "What do you want then, Ana? Let me guess. More money!" He saw Tucci relax against her desk. "I'll have the funds transferred to your account this afternoon." She paused before a comment on the line catapulted her into an upright position. "I don't have time to take down the information, you cross-dressing skank!" she growled. "Call Mario with the information. I'll take care of it from here." Tucci suddenly regained control, calming as she prepared to hang up. "I'm warning you, Ana. At some point, your threats are going to get you into more hot water than you could ever create for me. That's a promise, darling. Let me put it this way, you miserable soak: the next time you ask for anything, don't be surprised if I use my funds a whole other way. It doesn't cost that much for a sodden old drag queen to disappear these days." Before her threat could elicit a response, Anitra slammed the phone down and promptly made her way to the door, swinging it open onto Nate Dainty!

Nate looked at Anitra, her face flushed from the phone conversation.

"Nate Dainty." She smoothed out her crimson red micro-mini power suit, the blazer parted to reveal Tucci herself was wearing a limited-edition bedazzled *Find Him* tank top.

Nate stammered, "Is now a bad time?"

"Never, darling! Don't be silly." She welcomed the young man into her office. "Although I don't have much time to talk. I have auditions for a new film this afternoon."

"I won't be long." Nate entered the office, and Tucci paced to the cocktail bar, pouring herself and Nate a glass of water. "I just wanted to let you know that I saw your interview on the news last night. I'm glad you came forward to let everyone know about Myles Long's disappearance."

"So am I. I want you to feel the weight of the world is *off* your shoulders, Nate Dainty."

"I never really felt that this was a burden," Nate protested. "As I said before, I just happened into the situation."

"Of course," Tucci insisted. "But now that the police *are* aware of his disappearance, and as I've now invested thousands of dollars in a search team for Myles, you don't need to worry so much. I'm more than confident they'll recover him."

Was Anitra asking him to stop his part in the search? She leaned forward and grabbed Nate's hand. "We'll both get Myles Long back! I have no doubt about it. And when we do, I'll see to it that you reunite in a lavish setting most young lovers don't even dare dream of. I have a Summerland beach house on Padaro Lane that I scarcely ever use." She swiveled her chair and crossed her legs. "It would be the perfect spot for you two to enjoy a long weekend."

"That sounds incredible, Anitra," Nate agreed cautiously. "I am a little surprised."

"Oh?" Tucci's eyes searched him before leaning back in her chair.

"Especially after that video you received? How can you be so sure?" A thought crossed Nate's mind suddenly: Could all this be just a ploy for more publicity for Tucci's company? Nate's eyes widened at the thought: What if Myles Long was in Tucci's possession all along?

She let out a long-contained sigh and looked beyond Nate to the office door. Firmly, she said, "I want you to leave this to the professionals, now!" Nate started to protest, but Tucci raised her hand. "The last thing I want is another young man in a dangerous situation on account of this whole fiasco. Quite frankly, I've decided I like you, Nate Dainty. I would hate to see you harmed."

"I appreciate that, Anitra, really! But I enjoy helping."

"But it *is* a problem! I need you to agree to leave this to the authorities."

Nate agreed reluctantly. And Anitra's broad smile resurfaced.

"A toast to celebrate?"

"Celebrate?" Nate asked.

"Your safety," the producer said as she filled two flutes with chilled champagne. Nate turned the glass of champagne, trying to make sense of their conversation.

"I wish the toast was to *Myles Long's* safety. There's no reason to be concerned about mine."

Tucci clinked the young redhead's glass, took a sip and she eyed him. "Oh! But there is. I hate to eavesdrop, but I was downstairs earlier and overheard you and your young Hispanic friend discussing the peril you each found yourselves in last night. Making it evident to me your search is already causing more trouble than it's worth. Let's face it, Nate, you're a community college student, for crying out loud, not Miss Marple!"

"I'm closer than you or the authorities to finding Myles Long."

Her eyes grew cold. "You mean closer to getting yourself into *more* trouble. I've done my share of research on you, Nate. I can only imagine how not having parents can sometimes lead one astray, even put one into situations any child with a solid upbringing just wouldn't get involved in. How was it, again, that your parents perished?"

His hand began to shake, so he set the glass down. "It's still a mystery."

"It must have been hard, growing up without parents." Anitra poured on the sugar-coating.

"I was fortunate enough to be cared for by my uncle Carter and his friends."

"Yes, his *friends*." She smirked. "But still you must wonder what it would have been like, if your parents were still alive?"

Nate's face grew hot. "What does this have to do with Myles Long?"

"I'm only asking the same questions you yourself would ask in the course of one of your amateur manhunts."

"None of this has anything to do with Myles Long," Nate repeated, trying to remain calm despite her invading his private life.

"Tell me this." Tucci's emerald eyes glanced away. "Why is it when I ask questions about your personal life you become so defensive?"

"My childhood has little to do with why I came here today."

"Let me guess," Anitra said, "you were coming to learn more about me. Or perhaps to find out if I knew something you didn't. Why, then, can't I learn more about you? Isn't that fair?"

"I guess," Nate agreed, cooling off, "but there isn't much about me to tell."

"Come now," Tucci wheedled. "Let's see! Orphaned at the age of two! Raised by a gay uncle, who's well known and quite powerful in the industry. I can only *imagine* what life must have been like."

"What are you getting at?" Their meeting had only served to convince him Anitra Tucci was no ally in his search for Myles Long. However, before Tucci could answer his question, Mario entered with another bottle of champagne and a long white flower box.

"Looks like the start of a good day, Ms. Tucci." The assistant set the box on her desk and replaced the empty ice bucket with a freshly opened bottle of champagne.

"Yes, Mario, I agree." Tucci unfastened the ribbon around the box. "Champagne, flowers from yet another admirer, and a visit from my favorite twink, Nate Dainty."

The young redhead bristled at the word *twink* and refused the offer of more champagne. "I must be going."

"So soon?" Tucci pouted. "And here I thought we were going to have a *revealing conversation*."

"We already have," Nate countered. He exited the office quickly. Down the hallway, he leaned against the melamine wall to catch his breath. Suddenly, a bloodcurdling scream emerged from the office!

Without thinking, Nate made his way back, where the shaken exec sat at her desk in tears, Mario rubbing her shoulders.

"What happened?" Nate asked. He looked around to see the white box was now open and had been dropped onto the floor. Beside it was a long, dull flap of skin.

"I can't believe they did it!" Tucci wailed.

"Did what?" Nate neared the flesh on the carpet, examining it closely.

"Look! They cut off Myles Long's cock!" she howled.

A PACKED CASE!

Nate neared the large object with suspicion. A pungent odor filled the office. "First off," Nate said calmly, "This doesn't belong to Myles Long."

"How can you be sure?" Anitra asked, still looking away.

Nate used an unsharpened pencil from Tucci's desk to turn the severed member. "Unless, of course, he's an ardent sushi fan. Anitra, this appendage is nothing more than the siphon of a Geoduck Clam!"

Drying her eyes quickly and getting up to examine the object herself, she marveled at the size of the delicacy. "So it is!" Mario handed her a small white envelope from the box.

Nate leaned over to read the typed print: *Eat it, Bitch!*

She crumpled the note and paused before emitting her trademark trill. "An early delivery from that sushi shop around the corner. Mario, let's slice this up and give it a taste. Poor Mr. Yamamoto must be struggling for business."

"Looks like your Mr. Yamamoto knows *exactly* how you like *it*," Nate said before again exiting the office.

Making his way out of The Tavern, he mulled over the incident as he began dialing Beso. "Where are you?" Nate was happy to hear the voice of a friend. He'd just left the bar and was breathing fresh, clam-free air.

"We're on our way up to Ana Bender's at this moment,"

Beso panted as he sashayed up the second flight of stairs to the drag queen's third-floor condo.

"Great," Nate said, "because something tells me the sooner the better." He filled in his pal on the latest encounter with Tucci, including her special delivery.

"OMG!" Beso gasped. "I think I'd be scared shitless if I got a cock in the mail!"

"Only it wasn't really a cock, Beso. It was a clam, supposedly from some sushi shop around the corner."

"I think I'll stick to California rolls!"

"From the looks of the note attached, it seems like Tucci should as well. I'm not so certain it was the friendly gift she portrayed it to be. Anyway, something is definitely up between her and Ana Bender. When I first walked up to the office door, I heard her talking to Ana on the phone. Something about transferring money to Bender's account to keep her mouth shut."

"Shut about what?" Beso questioned.

"Exactly!" Nate said. "That's up to you and Jorge to find out!"

"Meanwhile, you'll get more info about Mac Needles from Manny Manos?" Beso teased.

"In a few hours." Nate laughed. "But first I need to swing by the gym for a quick workout. I don't want Manny to have texter's remorse!"

"As long as you have freckles on your ass and blazing red hair, I'm sure you and Manny Manos will get along fine, Nate Dainty!" Beso said before hanging up. Removing a napkin from his book bag, Beso dabbed the sweat off his brow and turned to his cousin, already perspiring in the late autumn heat wave. They were at Bender's apartment door, which was curiously ajar.

Knocking, Jorge pushed it open slightly and whispered "Ana?" into the condo. He then edged into the cool foyer.

Along one side of the hallway were two matching large sky blue suitcases. Motioning to Beso, he picked up a stack of paperwork balanced atop the luggage and saw a plane ticket to Puerto Vallarta for later that afternoon.

"Talk about taking the *dinero* and running," Jorge whispered. He heard the clicking of heels outside the door. Opening it, the pair came face-to-face with a large black man with a shaved head, wearing an orange and lime green kimono and massive wooden clogs.

"Ana? Is that you, girl?" Beso questioned.

The large queen smiled a telltale, crooked grin. "Well, well! If it isn't my drinking buds. I must apologize for my makeshift appearance. I wasn't expecting company. Come on in, fellas! I was just taking out the trash." Ana motioned the cousins to enter the modest, heavily mirrored, living room. He eyed the large bottle of vodka Jorge had brought. "And I can see you come bearing gifts."

"If you felt the way we did this morning, we figured you could use it." Jorge extended the bottle to Ana. "I just hope this time is okay for us to visit? Looks like you're headed out."

"This old girl needs a vacation! In a few hours I'm off to the airport, headed to sunny Mexico!"

"Fabuloso," Jorge replied. "To celebrate your little *viaje*, perhaps you have time for a farewell cocktail."

"With new friends? I'll make time!" Ana gushed, forgetting how the night ended. "But if it's not too much to ask, I could really use a ride to the airport, too."

"No *problema*." Jorge poured the vodka into three glasses. "Who doesn't love a visit to the airport?" Popping sliced lime into each glass, he made his way to the large red velvet sofa Ana had sprawled out on.

Beso took a glass, walking around the room, enjoying photos of Ana Bender then and now. "I have to say, Ana, I had no idea how many layers there have been in your career."

"Oh honey." Ana chugged down his first drink, the absence of cosmetics making him appear more gentle and sincere. "I've been around longer than Madonna. Luckily for me, darlin', black don't crack."

Jorge joined Beso admiring the photos. Many were of Ana in her Jen Bender days, performing on bar stages and posing with fans. Her severe New Wave look featured a hairstyle that was both tribal and intriguingly futuristic. Dark rouge had sharpened her cheekbones then, making her face all edges and streamlined.

"Who started this look, Ana? You or Tina?"

"Oh girl! *I'll* never tell." Ana cackled and set the empty glass down with a thud. "Unless, of course, you fill up this glass!"

Jorge winked at his cousin and turned back to the mini-bar to mix another.

Beso made his way to another series of photos. "Are all of these pictures from the mid-eighties?" He examined the flashy hairstyles, neon striping, and heavy makeup.

"That was my heyday, chile," the queen said, walking along with Beso. "These photos inspire me every day. It's how I can get up on that dirty old stage at *Sueños*!"

Beso looked at a photo of a young blond man posing with Ana, who was in a sedate outfit: a beige miniskirt and blazer with oversized shoulder pads. The spiky wild style had been replaced by conservative Jheri curls. Examining the photo, Beso noted Ana's oversized jewelry. "Was this during your *Dynasty* days?"

Ana smiled, set his glass down, and removed the photo from the wall. Running his hand affectionately along the picture frame, the often inebriated diva suddenly became quite somber. "Look at those shoulder pads," he said gently. "I definitely had a look going on that day, didn't I?"

"That blond hunk you're with is nothing to sneeze at either," Beso said. The man in the photo had loose, blond curls and sun-kissed skin; his white shirt was unbuttoned halfway down and tucked into a pair of tan dress pants.

"That old thing?" Ana winked at Beso. "He was my costar in a movie." He replaced the picture on the wall and then turned back to the couch. "Enough about me. Why don't you two come here and have a cocktail."

"A movie?" Beso eyed his cousin. "I had no idea you were a movie star, too!"

"Oh honey! I've been everything. But that movie never came to be."

Beso remained at the wall as Jorge approached. The man in the photo bore a striking resemblance to Myles Long! Could this be one of the few remaining photos of Chase Hastings, both wondered.

"Well, you two look set for stardom," Jorge flattered the diva. "What movie was it, anyway?"

"This is all old, boring stuff, boys. You don't wanna hear about it." Ana suddenly seemed humble.

"But we do!" Jorge returned to the couch, sat, and patted Ana's fat knee. "What was the movie?"

Ana's eyes suddenly became watery. "*Magic Afternoon.*"

Just as Beso was about to delve deeper, the phone rang. Ana leaned wearily back in the couch, searching under throw pillows until he found the cell.

"Hello!" Ana answered. "Yes…I'm alone," he lied, an index finger to his mouth to warn the cousins to be quiet. "It's about time you called!"

Jorge nodded at Ana and motioned that he and Beso would step out of the living room into the foyer.

"So!" Jorge whispered. "There *are* photos of Chase Hastings after all."

"Despite Mac's efforts, he wasn't able to destroy *every* memory of Chase, as he planned." Beso tittered. "Do you think Ana is involved in the kidnapping? How can we get some more answers before this flight?"

"Who said he's gonna even make the flight," Jorge replied, smiling at his cousin.

"*Jorgito!* What are you suggesting?"

"We can't let Ana Bender just flee the country the way Guy Carley did. If our leads keep vanishing into thin air, it won't be long before Myles Long is…!"

"Oh, *boys*," Bender called from the sofa.

The cousins reentered the living room to see Ana in even better spirits than before, holding out an empty glass. "I apologize for the interruption, but that was an old friend wishing me *bon voyage*. Speaking of which…I had better get going. I just remembered I need to make a quick stop at the bank before we head to LAX."

"No problema," Jorge agreed. "But first let's have one more drink!"

"Oooh! Twist my fat-girl arm," Ana flirted, batting his large brown eyes at the buff young Latino.

"You got it, *amiga*," Jorged winked, "but first I have to take a leak. Where's your *cuarto de baño*?"

"Just down that hall," Ana directed and turned to Beso. "Oh, doll! You just can't get enough of those photos of little old me! Can you?"

"I can't," Beso enthused. "You had so many amazing and fantastic looks!"

"I know, girl! Now I'm so big and scary. I need to lose the weight equal to a ten-year-old child! But it's gonna be hard with all those margaritas and carne asada tacos I'll be scooping up in Puerto Vallarta. I just hope those li'l brown chirrens don't mistake me for a big old *piñata* and start beating me with a stick!"

Jorge returned and quietly resumed his bartending duties. He filled up the glasses, but this time the cocktails were all slightly blue. "I thought I'd make my favorite drink before we hit the road! Something for you to remember us by in Mexico."

"So sweet!" Ana took a sip and his face brightened. "So delicious! What's it called?"

"Entrapment," Jorge boasted. "It's my own creation."

"So...*Magic Afternoon*." Beso returned to where they had all been prior to the phone call. "What a beautiful name. What was it about?"

"Oh girl," Ana smiled softly at Beso, "it was about hot man-on-man action!"

"You mean to tell me," Beso feigned shock, "*Magic Afternoon* was a porno?"

"It was supposed to be a kind of hybrid—more than sex. That's where I came in," Ana explained, shrugging. "But we know how *that* usually goes."

Ana finished his drink and slammed the glass down on the end table with a sense of finality. "Off we go." He started up from the couch. "I'd hate to miss my flight."

"I'll bet you can't wait to get to Mexico," Beso said, walking with Ana to the entry.

"I can't," Ana said determinedly, putting on a wide-brimmed hat and big, rhinestone-encrusted sunglasses. Beso and Jorge reached for his suitcases, but he stopped them, grabbing the smaller one from Beso. "You boys have done so much for me already, at least let me carry one bag."

Reluctantly, Beso released the bag to Ana, and the three made their way down to the ground floor. After putting the suitcases into Jorge's Mini Cooper hatchback, Beso shut the gate. Jorge moved the front seat for Ana to enter. "I'm sorry it's so cramped," he apologized.

"Can't complain about a free ride," the queen replied. "I'm just not sure I'll be able to get out once we get to the bank."

Fortunately Ana was able to exit the car with only a minor struggle when they arrived at the bank.

As the cousins waited in the car, Beso turned to Jorge. "What are you up to? I thought you said we couldn't let Ana Bender get to Mexico."

"She's not going to, cousin! Wait and see," Jorge said confidently, changing from his favorite dance channel to the classical station on the radio as the kimonoed queen returned with an envelope brimming full of cash.

"Let's go!" Ana squealed with more enthusiasm than ever. "I got everything I need. Oh yes I do!"

Jorge turned onto La Brea and headed to the airport. "I hope it's all right, Ana, I'm going to have to take surface streets!"

"I guess that's cool. But why?" Ana wondered.

"He may look big and strong," Beso patted Jorge on the back, "but my dear cousin is afraid of freeway driving."

"Carry on, sister!" Ana said, yawning slightly, "I know *all about that*."

Jorge gradually turned down the music. Leaning back into the next seat, Ana stretched out, her mouth widening into a long yawn. "I hope it won't offend anyone if I catch a few winks en route."

"Not at all." A sly smile crept across Jorge's face.

Within minutes, Ana Bender was snoring louder than a chainsaw, completely overwhelming the Mozart playing softly in the background.

Pulling to one side of the road, Jorge put the car in park and reached back to remove the envelope that Ana had clutched tightly when first leaving the bank. Inside was ten thousand dollars cash, along with a cashier's check for another five hundred thousand. Showing it to Beso, he said in a hushed tone, "I guess that was going to be *quite* a *trip*! But not like the trip Ana Bender's gonna have after a liter of vodka and four Tylenol PMs."

"Okay! Now what, Jorge? We have a huge drag queen in the back of the car who's not gonna be too pleased when he finds out he missed his flight."

"Follow me, cousin," Jorge replied, exiting the car, and making his way to the hatchback. "Remember how Ana insisted on carrying that suitcase? Didn't you find that a bit suspicious?"

"Absolutely," Beso agreed. "I always thought drag queens never carried anything larger than a cocktail purse!"

Raising the hatchback gate, Jorge reached for the case and began to undo the latches. "Why do you think that is?"

"We're about to find out," Beso said as he watched his cousin sift through the bag's contents.

Tossing aside bottles of concealer and some oversized panties, Jorge suddenly stopped as he lifted a large, gold-sequined halter top. Holding it up, he unraveled the fabric until it revealed a thick, rectangular, red plastic cartridge. He closely examined the bulky object.

"I know what that is," Beso said excitedly. "I learned about these in Gay Pop Culture class!"

"What the hell is it?" Jorge asked.

"I believe it's what they called a Betamax cassette," the plump lad enthused. "It came around before the time of the videocassette."

Turning the cassette around, Jorge stopped at the front of the tape and gasped. Eyes shining with excitement, he held the tape for Beso to read—the letters smeared in black marker ink on a thin piece of masking tape.

"*Magic Afternoon*!" the two squealed, in unison, shushing each other as they did.

A STEAMY ENCOUNTER

Fresh from a long workout at the gym, Nate pulled his orange Beemer into the Vapor Baths parking lot. The especially warm weather of the day had grown progressively cooler right after the sun set. With the convertible top locked into place, Nate caught a quick glance of his reflection in the rearview mirror before pulling on a gray hooded sweatshirt over his workout gear.

In less than a year, Vapor Baths had eclipsed the other area bathhouses by adding a top-of-the-line workout facility as well as private rooms that were a bit more upscale, and it offered services ranging from free wireless Internet to a full-service business conference room for those whose jobs followed them everywhere. When Nate entered the baths, he could see Vapor seemed to be living up to its rumored success, and that the list of amenities was growing in response. *Coming Soon*, a placard proclaimed, *18-Hole Glory Maze!*

"Hello there, young man," the cashier greeted him warmly, flashing a bright smile, as Nate approached. He was a lanky fellow with a fresh haircut, his neatly pressed polo and khaki shorts a sharp contrast to what went on behind closed doors. "Welcome to Vapor Baths. The *crème de la crème* of bathhouses, sex clubs—you name it! How can we be of service today?"

Nate found himself at a loss for words. Although he liked

to think of himself as worldly and ready for anything, this was his first visit to Vapor and, with his meeting with Manny Manos imminent, uncertainty made our redhead a trifle nervous.

Noting Nate's discomfort, the cashier relaxed, then nodded knowingly. "Sorry, bud, they make me say all that. First time?"

"Yes," Nate admitted, resting his gym bag on the counter.

"Fresh from the gym, I can see. Keep in mind, if you feel the need for a few emergency crunches, we have a first-class gym right here at Vapor. Everything at Vapor is first class. We're more than just a bathhouse."

"Do they make you say all that, too?"

"Look," the man admitted, "if I fail another Secret Shopper, my ass is fired! So what will it be?"

Nate opted to pay twenty dollars for the hourly locker, hoping that Manos had gotten a roomette. Undressing and donning an Egyptian-cotton bath towel, Nate shoved his belongings into the small locker and slipped on a pair of complimentary flip-flops. He walked from the locker room down a long hall tiled in opalescent gray slate. Soft music played, dim lights revealed glass panels along the walls, where water streamed down the glass in a continuous cascade. Touching the water, Nate was soothed. He could make out the aromas of jasmine and gardenia automatically piped in as he made his way into a slate-walled stall shower. Wow, Nate thought as he slipped off his towel and began to adjust the faucet's temperature and flow, this really is better than I thought.

Leaning back against the wall, Nate let the water glide gently across his face and chest, liberally applying the gel provided. The events surrounding Myles Long's disappearance had completely put him out of touch with his usual relaxed SoCal state of existence. And if Manny Manos failed to show, Nate thought, at least he'd be chilled out.

Lost in thought, it took Nate a moment to realize that the sensation of his own hands rubbing the shower gel had multiplied.

Opening his eyes, he saw the other hands rubbing him down belonged to a handsome, olive-skinned Latino, with thick body hair matted by the water. Nate blinked the water out of his eyes and refocused, this time up on the close-cropped fade haircut and goatee of his shower companion.

"Need help soaping up?" the guy asked, then slid fully into the stall.

Need help soaping up? Nate's eyes brightened in recognition: that was Manny Manos' famous line as the car-wash attendant in *The Straight Shooter*!

"Absolutely," Nate agreed. He poured more shower gel into Manny's hands.

"So you *are* Jorgito and Beso's *amigo*?" Manny's boyish smile revealed his trademark capped tooth. "From their description, I figured it had to be you."

"I'm Nate," he confessed, feeling Manny's cock against his body.

"Nice to meet you, Nate." Manny's soaped-up chest rubbed against Nate's in the tight stall. Manny slipped his tongue into Nate's mouth and kissed him gently as both cocks grew erect against each other. Manny began to kiss Nate's neck, and his left hand trailed to his ass and pulled apart his cheeks in anticipation. "I take it you're up for this?"

"Yes," Nate said, surprised by his reaction. "I've been pretty horned-up ever since, well, ever since the day I met Myles Long."

"Fuck yeah," Manny growled in agreement. "That dude is *pinche* hot! But he's got nothing on you. Damn, look at all those freckles!"

The two locked lips. Nate could feel the heat rising and he dropped the shower gel bottle. He gripped the stud's hard-on and began rubbing it. Manos leaned back and winked. "Slow down, man. You don't wanna rush it, do you?"

"Not at all." Logic made him question why he had these

feelings for Manny, when he'd already invested so much time in tracking down Myles Long. Another part of him, less logical, said it was okay. After all, he was young, and had needs.

Between long kisses, Manny said, "So, did you get a room?"

"No. Did you?"

The bartender/porn star shrugged. "Locker."

Nate perked up, undaunted. "I'm sure it's not too late, I could always upgrade to a Jack-Off Suite."

"Too damn *caro*, man," Manny shook his head at the expense they'd incur. "Tell you what. In the steam room, there's an area in the back with two long benches. No one ever sees them because of all the steam. I'll go get condoms and lube. You wait in there." He grabbed Nate's left buttock. "And we can pick up exactly where we left off."

Nate agreed, then regained his senses to add, "And don't forget, we also have to discuss Mac Needles' whereabouts."

"After I get what's coming to me." Manny smiled and walked out of the stall.

Nate could still feel his pulse racing as he dried himself off and went to the attendant to get a new dry towel. As Nate made his way to the steam room, he flirted with the men beginning to crowd the hallways and rooms. To the left of a small screening room, showing a movie even Nate hadn't seen before, was a beveled glass door leading to the steam room.

Nate felt the soothing effects of the steam as he entered and found the left corner Manos had directed him to. Although out of view from the rest of the steam room, the fog was beginning to dissipate and he made out a couple near the beveled-glass entrance. In their late thirties, they were making out, even unfastening their towels.

This is like a peepshow, Nate thought as he watched the two stroke each other off. Moaning in ecstasy, both ejaculated onto the floor, dabbed each other dry, and exited.

Thank heavens for flip-flops, Nate thought. Neatness freak that he was, Beso would wig out if he were here.

The sound of hot water pumping out of the valves began to dominate the empty room. Nate leaned back and slowly breathed in and out, the steam clouding his vision, covering him in vapor. The sneak preview earlier with Manos had him ready for more. Of course, all in the interest of finding out more about Mac Needles, Nate half convinced himself as the warm mist grew to a thick, impenetrable fog. He made out the dark shadow of Manos headed toward him.

"You made it!" Nate dropped his towel and resumed where they'd left off, the stubble of Manny's goatee chafing his tender lips. Nate attempted to take more control and thrust his own tongue into Manos' mouth, kissing him deeply. Despite this, he still found himself letting go, Manny's tongue sliding to the roof of his mouth, exploring. Nate felt himself steered toward the wall as Manos pulled his own towel off and began to tease Nate's hole with the head of his cock. Holding him by one side, Nate leaned away from Manos before he felt his neck guided downward by Manny's gentle yet forceful hand. Sliding down, Nate dropped to his knees and began servicing the large shaft, wrapping his lips around the mushroom head before taking him deep into his mouth.

The heavy, almost synthesized, sound of the emitting steam continued to escalate and blocked out the music from the hall. He could faintly hear moaning from above as his hands explored the chiseled, hairy chest of his newfound fuck-bud. Without hesitation, Nate took the tool deep to the back of his throat, savoring every grunt of satisfaction he could make out.

Looking up, Nate made out the hairy forearms reaching up and turning him around, pushing him gently against the wall, and he heard the condom slip over Manos' cock with a snap. He could feel Manny's hand slide closer to his hole, the cool gel of the lube sliding up into him with each rub. Before he could turn to face Manos one more time, he felt the head of Manny's cock fully enter and move him forward, his chest close against the tiled wall.

"You need this, don't you?" he whispered softly as he teased Nate with each jab, his chest heaving in long breaths against Nate's back.

"Yes," Nate said, feeling the pressure of Manny's cock plunge again into his hole, his legs weakening as Manos continued to ride him. His chest held up by Manos' forearm, he was repositioned to the bench, his knees resting on the first level as he began to now completely enjoy every movement of Manny's shaft, finding himself wanting it more each time the stud withdrew. Eagerly, Nate began to rub his own cock. With each thrust of Manny's cock, the tension in his groin continued to swell.

"That's right. You wanna come?" Manny asked deeply, his breath hot against Nate's ear. "Huh?"

"Yeah," Nate moaned and, by surprise, he felt Manny grab his hand away from his cock as he continued to drive into him deeply.

"Come," he heard Manos grunt as his own hand now guided Nate's. The two rubbed Nate's cock in full, but rapid strokes as Manos commanded again, "Come!"

With each push of Manny's cock, Nate could feel the shots of semen bursting from his own dick. Crying out, he felt the tight spasm of his ejaculation climb to one final shot on the first level of the bench. His body covered with sweat and damp steam, he felt Manny's thrusts grow more rapid as he also groaned, emitting a low gasp as he removed his cock, snapped the condom off, and shot his load all over Nate's back. Lying on top of him, crouched over the bench, Nate could feel the damp hairy chest rub against his smooth back as Manos kissed his neck lightly. The charged jets of the steam came to a sudden halt, leaving only the echoes of the couple's heavy breathing within the tiled chamber. Slowly, the heavy fog began to dissipate.

"That was amazing," Nate said afterward, wiping his brow with the towel. He could hear a low moan of agreement as he attempted to dry his face. "And definitely a fair price for you telling me what you know about Mac Needles."

When he turned around, the clearing steam revealed a body next to him similar to Manos', but not exactly so. His eyes darted through the mist, noting that while the dark goatee surrounding the man's mouth and the close-cropped fade he had witnessed earlier on Manos were there, the man he had just had sex with was *not* Manny Manos! His eyes now scanned not the soft, toying eyes of Manny Manos, but the dark, haunted eyes of Mac Needles!

"What would you like to know about me, Firecrotch?" Mac asked, with a cruel smirk.

BIENVENIDOS AMIGOS

"What are you two doing here?" Hans asked as Jorge and Beso pulled into the Daintys' garage. The aging houseboy stood in the garage doorway, squinting at the Mini Cooper, as he pulled his short terrycloth robe closer around his body.

"We need your help, Hans," Beso whispered, quietly closing the car door. The two entered the house on tiptoe.

"By all means, come right on in. Where is Nathan? I've had a midnight snack of chocolate cake and soy milk waiting for him since he left for the gym, hours ago."

"Well, don't mind me if I help out with that!" Beso said. "I never could pass up a good piece of chocolate cake." He entered the kitchen, licking his lips at the tall dome of dessert.

"Beso! Do you mind?" Jorge snapped. "We have more going on here right now than your insatiable appetite."

Hans sat at the kitchen table, scowling, and reapplied an ice pack to his still aching shoulder. "And you, George, are making yourself a most undesirable guest. I understand your trailer went up in flames, but this coming and going as you please, insulting my cooking, and parking in our garage like you own the place simply has to stop! Wait until Uncle Carter returns from his business trip. If you weren't Nathan's good friend, I'd—"

"Just hold one minute, *vieja*," Jorge interrupted. "We're

doing this for Nate. It's not like I drive around town collecting three-hundred-pound drag queens for kicks."

Hans looked at Beso for answers. Obligingly, the plump cousin sat down to a fresh-sliced piece of the cake.

"Hans, what Jorge's saying is true! We need your help! We went to see Ana Bender because we thought he had clues to Myles Long's whereabouts."

"But, as it turns out," Jorge continued, "we found more than we had bargained for. Ana had just blackmailed Anitra Tucci for five hundred grand. Girlfriend was hitting the road, headed for Puerto Vallarta this afternoon."

"We couldn't let him leave without finding out exactly what he knew about Myles Long."

"Then go back to his house and find out what you need," Hans snapped, pausing for a long yawn. "But leave me out of it."

"See, that's the problem, Hans," Beso challenged. "You're the only one we can turn to right now."

"How is that?" Hans suddenly pulled the plate of half-eaten cake toward him and snatched the fork out of Beso's hand. "I've had enough trouble from the two of you. The *fiesta*, as your people say, is over."

Beso and Jorge looked at each other and laughed. "That's perfect, Hans! Do you know any other Spanish?"

"Excuse me?" he snapped back.

"Actually," Beso joked, "it's more like 'Eck KYOO me.'"

Jorge doubled over in laughter.

"It's time for my beauty rest. You two go off and do whatever it is you want with this Ana Bender. I'm going to bed."

"Don't you see, Hans, this is where *you* come in!" Jorge said excitedly. "This is how *you* can help Nate Dainty solve this manhunt."

"Jorge and I both know how much you've been worrying about Nate." Beso attempted to appeal to Hans' motherly side.

"The more you help us with Ana Bender, the sooner Nate will spend nights at home, enjoying your delicious meals and keeping you company while Uncle Carter is away on business."

The houseboy rolled his eyes but was softened. "It *has been* awfully lonely here lately. Without Nathan around, I've been tossing leftovers into the trash. Such a waste!"

The cousins eyed Hans, pleading, before he grudgingly caved in.

"Oh, all right, you two! What do you want me to do?"

"First off," Jorge returned to business, "we have the issue of your Spanish-speaking abilities."

"Yes." Beso pulled out a sheet of paper from his shirt pocket. "To make this transition easier, Jorge and I have put together a list of conversational Spanish to help you and Ana Bender pass the time."

Hans apprehensively took the sheet of paper, and read, "*Bienvenido, amigo*?"

Beso waved his hand dismissively. "When Ana wakes up for breakfast, you need to say it with more fervor, and more meaning." He took a step back and crossed his arm over his chest, then extended it in a bold move. "*Bienvenido, amigo!*"

"Yes! Like that," Jorge agreed eagerly.

"What—are—you—two—talking—about?" Hans asked.

"Don't you see, Hans," Beso encouraged, sitting down again next to the aged houseboy. "The Spanish Colonial architecture of this house, the fact that it faces the canyon and *not* the city, not to mention the recent heat wave we've been having, all make this house the perfect resort for Ana to wake up in."

"You mean you want me to pretend this is a Puerto Vallarta resort?" Hans scoffed, stood up, and fussed about the kitchen.

"For one day only," Jorge said. "Long enough for us to buy time to wrap up this manhunt."

"What am I going to say," Hans asked, "when Ms. Bender wants to go to the beach?"

"Tell him there's been a stingray attack, an oil spill, jellyfish invasion, I don't know," Jorge replied. "I know you'll think of *something*."

"With the amount of pills Jorge spiked his drink with, he should sleep through the night," Beso explained. "All you have to do, when he wakes up in the morning, is what you do best: make a delicious breakfast, show him about his private suite, and let him lounge in the comfort of the infinity pool."

"And when in doubt, keep those Bloody Marys coming!" Jorge added.

"Where," Hans questioned, "do you expect me to keep Miss Tons-Of-Fun?"

Beso shrank back. "We were hoping…he could stay in Uncle Carter's room?"

"You've lost your minds! All right, bring him in. But I'm giving you *one day* to get this all wrapped up. If that big queen is in Mr. Dainty's bed when he gets back from New York, I'll be out on my wonderfully contoured *ass*."

"It's a deal," Jorge agreed excitedly, rushing forward to hug and then wisely deciding to settle on a handshake with the houseboy. "I take back almost every bad thing I've ever said about you."

"I wish *I* could say the same." Hans leaned back, crossed his arms, and pursed his lips. "You can do all the heavy lifting. There's no way I'm gonna break my back."

The cousins ran out to the Mini Cooper and slowly dragged the large diva into the kitchen and down a long hallway leading to Carter Dainty's master suite. Snoring and moaning incoherently, the large man drooled all over his kimono as Beso and Jorge groaned beneath his weight. After propping Ana on one side of the bed, they slowly slid him into an upright position, pulled back the covers, and rested his head against a thick, down-filled pillow.

Turning off the lights, they closed the door and returned

to the kitchen where Hans was loading the dishwasher, looking down the hallway with concern. "That queen looks strangely familiar."

"Perhaps an old trick?" Jorge asked as Hans rolled his eyes in disapproval.

"Now that I'm helping you, you can tell me what's happened to Nathan."

"Nate had a date," Beso answered quickly. Hans stood up from his chore and looked at the plump lad, suspicious that he was being toyed with.

"He didn't mention that earlier. He said he was headed off to the gym."

"It was a guy he met at the gym," Jorge covered. "You know! They were just grabbing a drink after an intense workout session."

"How I long for those days," Hans said sadly as he flopped back into the dining room chair. "All the good times! The hot dates! The sudden attractions."

"Was there a lot of cruising going on in those covered wagons?" Jorge asked.

"I'm not the dinosaur you think I am, George," Hans said. "In fact, I was just telling Nate last night that I was once up for a starring role in one of Mac Needles and Chase Hastings' feature films."

"I hardly consider Assistant Fluffer a starring role," Jorge said dismissively.

"That's fabulous, Hans," Beso said encouragingly. "Which part?"

"I was supposed to be in a movie called *Magic Afternoon*, but before they shot my scene, well, that was when Chase Hastings tragically died."

The two looked at each other in surprise. "Maybe that's why Ana Bender looks familiar," Jorge exclaimed. "He was involved in the movie, too."

"Was that the last time you pursued a career in porn?" Beso asked.

"Yes. My last hurrah…" Hans' voice trailed off as he closed the dishwasher door.

"Then he went back to being a regular off-the-camera slut," Jorge added.

"It's too bad you weren't more involved in the filming, Hans," Beso continued, ignoring Jorge's dig, "because we have a feeling that *Magic Afternoon* may have something to do with Ana's connection with Anitra Tucci."

"Anitra Tucci?" Hans repeated, his eyes glazed over for a moment. "No! I don't remember her name *ever* being mentioned."

"Some way, somehow, *something* about *Magic Afternoon* is connected to Tucci Productions," Jorge said.

"But what?" Beso pondered, then his eyes lit up. "Hans! You wouldn't happen to have an old Betamax player by any chance, would you?"

Hans laughed at the young chubby gay. "I haven't had a Betamax player in years."

"We have to find one," Beso continued, "or else we'll never know what's on the tape Bender was taking with him to Mexico."

"Well, good luck, my friends," Hans said discouragingly. "I don't think there's a single Betamax in existence after The Bolt held its famous Betamax Burning festival back in the late eighties."

"Betamax Burning?" Jorge repeated. "Now I've heard everything."

"Oh, it was clever at the time. The Bolt had just remodeled and it was New Year's Eve, 1989. 'Say Good-bye to All Things Eighties' was the slogan. If you brought something in that was just So Eighties: a 'Just Say No' pin, large shoulder pads, or a Members Only jacket, then you could enter the club free. But if you brought in a Betamax, you would go to the front of the line."

"Great. Since we have no place to play this archaic tape, I guess we'll just have to rely on your memories of what *Magic Afternoon* was all about."

"I wish I could help with that." Hans sadly poured them cups of tea. "The storyline and characters of *Magic Afternoon* were top secret. The only two people who knew the plot and story were Needles and Hastings. The rest of us only knew our own scenes." Hans set down the teapot and gazed off again, recalling another time. "In fact, the only thing I can still remember was my own first line."

"'The more the merrier'?" Jorge wisecracked, sipping the aromatic tea.

"Actually," Hans said, "It was 'Need help soaping up?'"

Beso spat out his tea, dropped his cup into the saucer. and let out a loud gasp.

Jorge shushed his cousin. "What exactly was your role in that movie, Hans?"

"It was a young and sexy role, of course," the houseboy said fondly. "I was a hunky, horny Swedish car-wash attendant, hoping to rub down more than cars!"

"That sounds exactly like—" Beso began.

"Manny Manos' role in *The Straight Shooter*!" Jorge finished.

"And his first line, too!" Beso added.

The houseboy looked at them, unconvinced. "Well, I realize it wasn't the *most original dialogue* in the world. It's probably been used since then."

"Don't you see, Hans!" Jorge continued, "This could be more than coincidence?"

"Maybe," Beso pondered, "Tucci *stole* the storyline of *Magic Afternoon* for *The Straight Shooter* and tried to pass it off as her own."

"Not realizing," Jorge added excitedly, "that Mac Needles would exact revenge by kidnapping Myles Long."

"It makes sense," Hans agreed. "But you won't know for sure until you see that tape."

"Wait a minute," Jorge recalled, "Nate said that Anitra Tucci had a lot of old audio-visual equipment in her office. He said she kept it so she could play old movies when she needed to unwind."

"And pirate old forgotten films at the same time," Beso said.

"Maybe she actually saved one of those old Betamax players from the blaze." Jorge jumped up, grabbing his car keys off the table. "There's only one way to find out!"

"I'm so exhausted!" Beso complained, leaning against the kitchen table. "Don't tell me we're headed to The Tavern."

"You can rest once we have answers, cousin," Jorge retorted. "In the meantime, we're going to work day and night until we find Myles Long!"

Emitting a weak moan, the plump cousin pushed his way from the chair and eyed Hans tiredly. "Whatever you do, Hans, don't let Bender out of the house. Keep that lush juiced up good. Deal?"

"Deal, you silly boys."

With that parting, the two pulled out of the garage and Hans waved good-bye.

Checking his watch and seeing that it was now past midnight, Hans called Nate's cell phone number, surprised to hear his voicemail pick up suddenly. "Well," he said as he hung up the phone, opting not to leave a message, "It sounds like Nathan's having more than just *drinks* with this lad from the gym."

A sudden loud crash made Hans drop the phone. The sound was from behind Uncle Carter's bedroom door! Slowly making his way down the hall, he heard heavy movements and moans before the door slowly opened to reveal a large black man in nothing other than boxers and a pair of false eyelashes. "Oh, my head," he murmured as he stepped out of the doorway.

Standing up straight, Hans extended his arm with a false sense of bravado.

"Bienvenido, amigo," he bellowed. "Welcome to Hansito's Hideaway!"

PART FOUR: CHASE HASTINGS

PART FOUR · CHASE HASTINGS

ROPED IN!

"Mac Needles!" Nate cried in disbelief. "But I was supposed to meet Manny Manos here!"

Mac grabbed Nate's wrists and twisted them behind his back, reaching for a rope he'd brought into the steam room. "You can scream and holler all you want, you little snoop! It's not gonna do any good. Not now, at least."

"Are you insane?" Nate challenged. "This is a public bathhouse! You can't hold me hostage here. Some horny guy is sure to be here any minute."

"It won't be Manny Manos. He's gone. Amazing what a five-hundred-dollar bribe will do for a little hustler like him! Don't worry, he sends his regards. I'll let him know he missed out on a nice piece of ass."

Nate struggled to escape Needles' grip. Needles released his arms, which Nate realized were now tightly bound.

"Besides," Needles continued, "As far as anyone knows, the steam room's temporarily closed for repairs."

"You can't do that!"

"You can when you're the owner," Needles winked mockingly, "a little fact you and your little friends couldn't quite figure out." He grabbed a towel and dried himself off, tossing it to the side as he stared at Nate, now helpless and in his possession. "I tried telling you to mind your own business, Nate Dainty. I guess my warnings weren't intimidating enough for you to leave me alone."

"I'd love to," Nate said, "once I see Myles Long is alive and well."

Mac laughed. The lack of steam made Mac now appear more clearly: the former star had not aged a bit. Mac stood, covered in perspiration. "After the note I left with your chubby little pal, what I did to Guy Carley, and after roughing up Hans, why didn't you stop looking?" He turned back to Nate and examined him closely. "Anyone in their right mind would have called the police, and then run for cover."

Nate sat on the bench and felt a calm sweep over him as the dark and dangerous captor suddenly seemed so human. "I've learned quite a bit about you," Nate admitted. "Maybe I'm crazy. But I don't believe you're as dangerous as you want everyone to believe."

"Oh?" Mac moved closer to Nate threateningly, but the intense heat of his body was now difficult to deny. "What makes you think that?"

"Well," Nate said as casually as possible, "you haven't seriously hurt anyone yet." He slid away from Mac and attempted to ignore the physical need that suddenly seemed to supersede all sleuthing.

"Not that *you* know of," Mac challenged.

Nate shook his head in disbelief. Even now, knowing that the man he had been with was Mac Needles, he still found himself wanting more.

"And from what I *have* learned, Mac," Nate continued, "what happened to you, years ago when Chase died, it left your life empty."

Mac let out a long breath. He sank onto the bench beside Nate and stared ahead. Nate could see his eyes well with tears.

"I can only imagine what it must have been like, to be so in love with someone, to have so many dreams of the future,"

Nate admitted. "I've never felt that before, but I know if I did I wouldn't want to lose it ever."

"I *don't* want to lose it," he confessed. "If you only knew how bad it feels. To carry all that emptiness around for all those years."

Nate said gently, "You can't bring him back."

"You don't know what he did to me!" Mac said. "How much he hurt me."

"It was a car accident," Nate reasoned. "You have to let go, get on with your life."

"That's what I did," he argued. "Look around. I created all this: this gay playland, so maybe one day someone else could have the same exciting life I once had."

"*You can* have that again," Nate encouraged, "but it won't be the same, Mac. Myles Long isn't Chase Hastings." Despite Mac's quizzical expression, he went on, "You can't hold Myles captive and try to make him someone he's not."

"I already came to the same realization." Mac smiled weakly. "I can't tell you how angry it made me, first seeing him up on the screen. Then on billboards and in magazines. If it weren't for all the therapy I had in the nineties, I probably would've killed him by now. Just to relieve myself."

"That's exactly what I was afraid of," Nate confessed.

"And you aren't anymore?"

"To be honest," Nate revealed, "when I first saw that video you sent Anitra Tucci, I was worried."

"That was my goal!" Needles admitted. "What was it that changed your opinion?"

"Well, aside from the fact that we've just had the hottest sex I've had in months?" Nate said with a laugh. "I guess the first real clue was when Tucci received that Geoduck Clam, trying to make her think you'd chopped off Myles' cock. If you really were the madman everyone made you out to be, you would have sent the real thing."

"Your instincts aren't so bad, after all," Mac said. "You're right about one other thing."

"What?" Nate asked, curiously.

Mac put his arm around him. "Our sex *was* incredible! I don't know about you, but I definitely needed it." Nate caught his breath. The warmth of Mac's body against his renewed his excitement. Mac rose and helped Nate up. "One good thing's come out of this…debacle," he said, a sly smile crossing his face. "I've been trying all week for Myles to put out. Now I don't need him! I sure never had *those* problems with Chase!"

Nate smiled, too. "Untie me and take me to Myles Long, and all is forgiven."

"Not so fast, Firecrotch. There are a few loose ends I need to tie up before I can untie *you*."

"But," Nate said with bewilderment, "I thought we'd come to an understanding."

"We have," Mac agreed, pushing the two benches upright. "But there's *much more* to this than I think you realize." Needles pulled the benches up and pressed against the wall. The wall slowly gave way to a long corridor.

"A secret room?" Nate's heart raced in panic. Perhaps he'd reacted prematurely in deciding that Needles was a gentle giant!

"Of course," Needles remarked casually, "and a soundproof one at that." He quickly pushed Nate into the chamber and latched the rope binding his hands to a small hook on the wall. "That," he said with satisfaction, "ought to keep you out of trouble a while. Maybe I'll just keep you here as my sex slave. That would really help me get over the pain of the past."

"You wouldn't! That's not the type of guy you are!"

"I guess you'll find out," Mac challenged. "In the meantime, I'd like you to solve a little puzzle."

"What's that?" Nate asked nervously.

"I'd like you to decide who you were *really* looking for on this little manhunt, Nate Dainty. Were you looking for Myles Long? Or did you somehow find yourself looking for me?"

Nate was silenced by the question. His captor smiled knowingly and gave him a quick kiss on the lips before leaving the secret room, sliding the wall shut once again.

His eyes adjusted to the darkness, and Nate could make out that the room was completely bare, with the exception of a few wood beams and old nails that littered the floor. There must be some way I can get out of this, he thought as he worked to pull his roped hands free. If I can just get off of this hook, I'll be able to explore.

Standing on tiptoes, leaning forward, Nate could feel the hook slowly pull out from the wall. Putting his entire body into it, he broke free, stumbling forward into the corridor, his left foot stepping on one of the old nails. Stepping back, Nate allowed his eyes to adjust more, his feet brushing the floor to prevent another puncture. Frantically twisting his hands, he managed to turn his left hand toward the base of the knot. He dug his nails into the rope, ripping in small, quick motions, until the knot gradually gave way. He shook his hands to let the blood flow through them again.

I can't make out where this room ends, he thought, hands carefully out as he walked in darkness. He came to a steel wall, felt along the surface, and located a small handle. Pulling it up made a small wall panel give way slightly. As he pushed it open, a faint light emerged, displaying a small room. Kneeling, he made his way in. His eyes adjusted to the light that entered through a skylight high above. The moon's soft glow revealed a small bedroom, furnished sparsely with a tall wardrobe and dresser. A full-length mirror stood beside a double bed, where a figure was sleeping.

In small steps, our Naked Redhead made his way over to the figure. As he approached, the figure suddenly turned in sleep, emitting a grunt, and his head rolled onto the pillow that was bathed in moonlight. His eyes opened slightly. He sat up, apparently realizing he wasn't alone. It was then that Nate once again came in contact with the sweet bedroom-eyed gaze of Myles Long!

A FINE MESS!

It was just after two a.m. when Beso and Jorge arrived at The Tavern, its bustling activity grinding to a halt as Security reminded the remains of the crowd that "last call" had already come and gone.

"Great! Now what?" Beso pondered.

"Follow my lead, cousin," Jorge commanded as they approached the entrance, which was blocked by a thickly muscled, crew-cut blond in a black V-neck T-shirt, fidgeting with a large key ring attached to the belt on his jeans. Gazing at the man's massive build, Jorge's eyes stopped at his left pectoral, where a small, brushed nickel name tag displayed the word *Security*.

"Sorry, boyth! Bar is clothed," he lisped. Jorge and Beso both did a double take at the guard.

"If it's all right, señor," Jorge said, in his most courteous tone, "I need to go back into the bar just a moment. I left my cell phone in the bathroom!"

"He can't *live* without it, Officer," Beso supported him, enthusiastically.

The security guard examined them, then stepped aside to allow them in. "Make it fatht!"

The cousins hurried in and headed to the back of the bar, where the stairwell led to Tucci's offices. "I had no idea," Beso quipped, "that this bar was clothed!"

"Oh stop!" Jorge said. "He let us in!"

The hallway door was unlocked, and they entered quietly, listening for any sounds of activity. The door to the immediate right was an office for the bar manager, and was just slightly ajar, the clanking of coins audible as a manager leaned over a cash drawer. They made their way past him and the door to Tucci's office at the end of the hall. To their chagrin, the door was locked.

"What *mala* luck!" Beso was exasperated. "Let's get out of here and try again tomorrow."

"Hold on." Jorge focused on the challenge before them. "I have one more idea."

"Where's Nate when we need him?" Beso complained. "Here I thought he got us into deep enough trouble. But look at you."

Jorge revealed his plan: Beso would gush over the security guard's hot body and attempt to remove the key ring from his belt loop.

"If we both start feeling him up," Jorge said, "with the seductive wiles of Tangelo and Ramirez in full effect, he won't even know what hit him!"

It took a modicum of persuading, and even an offer to buy Beso a late-night snack at the local *taquería*, but Beso finally agreed.

"Well, boyth, find the phone?" the guard asked, revealing a friendly smile.

"We did, and we thank you again," Jorge said.

Beso grabbed the guard's arm.

"Sweet Jesus!" he squealed. "You must have been sent from heaven above, to have biceps like this! *Jorgito*, feel these arms!"

"Increíble!" Jorge gushed. "You must work out like *todo el día*!"

The guard blushed, admitting that a combination of Midwest

farmer genes and a daily three-hour gym regimen did the trick. As Jorge inquired about his technique, Beso poked the guard's rock-solid abs, too.

"It's like your chest is made of Teflon," the plump lad marveled.

Grinning proudly, the guard flexed and posed.

Beso quickly unlatched the keys, took a quick feel of the man's gluteus, and gave Jorge a wink.

"Oops! Look at the time," Jorge said quickly. "Thanks again for your help, *guapo!*"

"Ciao!" Beso said, the keys safely inside his pocket.

Striding with careful confidence until they were at the corner, the two ran for a full block of Santa Monica Boulevard and slowed to catch their breath.

"Talk about 'young, dumb, and full of…workout routines'!" Beso panted. "Now! Let's get that snack you tempted me with."

The pair traveled a half block to the open-all-night taco stand, where Beso greedily ordered a Guacamole Combo Platter, and a large horchata to drink.

"Qué lástima! Why don't you milk me for *all* I'm worth, Beso!" Jorge complained as he doled out money to the cashier.

"You and Nate both owe me big time. This Guacamole Combo Platter is just the appetizer." Beso slurped down the large pink horchata, dabbing his brow with a paper napkin.

Jorge dialed Nate's number a second time, frowning as he hung up. "Still no answer," he said, his face furrowed in concern. "I'm going to send him a quick text just in case, to let him know what's going on."

"I'm sure he's having a whale of a time with Manny Manos," Beso teased. "I mean, how could you not? He's only one of the hottest porn stars in the business!"

"I suppose—if you're into that type," Jorge murmured before he dialed another number. "I'm going to try Hans and see if all is well with Ana Bender."

On the second ring, Hans picked up.

"*Buenos días*! Thank you for calling Hansito's Hideaway!"

"Hans?" Jorge asked in disbelief.

On the other line, Hans' forced smile clouded with anger as he left the kitchen and stepped out onto the patio. "I can't believe what you two got me into!" the aged houseboy complained. "Soon as you left, Ana Bender woke up from his *siesta* and was ready for a *fiesta*!"

"We hope you're keeping him entertained?" Jorge asked.

"I'm doing what I can, honey," Hans said. "Right now, I'm giving him a Hansito Hideaway Spa Treatment, special facial mask, and soothing foot soak, all served with a complimentary Hideaway Margarita."

"*Perfecto!*" Jorge marveled, "I knew you had it in you."

"Whatever 'it' is," Hans said with disdain, as he slid back into the kitchen, his tone changing. "All right then, sir! We look forward to seeing you and your partner next Friday evening. We'll be *sure* to have your room ready!"

Hans clicked off the phone and turned to his guest, Ana Bender, who lay sprawled out on a kitchen chair, his mud-covered face in a blissful expression as he enjoyed the soothing effect of the eucalyptus foot soak.

"Another reservation," Hans explained as he sat down next to Bender. "It seems you're enjoying all the perks of the Hideaway so far, señor," Hans said, relieved that he had so far fooled his house guest. "Would you like another margarita while the mask dries?"

"Honey! I thought you'd *never* ask," the queen drawled, his lips tightening as the caked-on face mask began to crackle.

"You were telling me all about your adventures in Hollywood," Hans prompted as he squeezed fresh lime juice into the glass. "Being here in Puerto Vallarta must seem like small potatoes compared to all *that* action."

"Wish I could remember the trip here," Ana said dazedly.

"The one time I buy first-class tickets, and I can't even remember what I had for dinner."

"Not to worry! It won't hold a candle to the meals you'll enjoy here at Hansito's Hideaway."

"I can't wait," Ana moaned. "In the meantime, you wouldn't happen to have any Fritos, would you?"

"Of course." Hans took a break from preparing the margarita to rummage through the pantry. "I have a fresh family-size bag here, with your name on it."

"Perfecto," Ana said. "Though I should take it easy on the snack food. I'm hoping that during my stay here I can get myself back into shape. If only you'd seen me twenty years ago…"

"Join the club, honey," Hans agreed as he set out the bowl of chips. "That's what I tell *all* the younger boys who come in. Enjoy it while you can." He looked at the queen brightly, briefly forgetting all the deception surrounding the visit.

"That's so right, and I *did* enjoy it, too," Ana said thoughtfully, removing his feet from out of the soak and lightly toweling them off.

"Then you wake up one morning and, suddenly," Hans plopped the margarita in front of Ana Bender, *"everything's* changed."

"I remember the day," Ana exclaimed with a dry laugh. "A day I'd like to forget! Believe me! But I don't think I ever will." Staring at his freshly soaked feet, he wiggled his toes and took a sip. "Delicious," he commented as Hans sat down next to him, helping himself to the bowl of chips.

"Me, too," Hans said, memories washing over him. "All of a sudden I couldn't get a dancing job if my life depended on it. Which is why I ended up here, in fabulous Puerto Vallarta," he added, surprised by his newfound cunning ability. "I went from aging in dog years in WeHo to aging in…maybe…*cat years* here. I guess there are *worse places*."

"There are, Hansito," the queen confirmed. "Trust me, I've

been there. I can still remember that morning, and getting that phone call." He took another sip, crossed his legs, and turned toward Hans confidingly. "I remember the sound of desperation at the other end of the line."

"Friend of yours?" Hans questioned.

"He *was* a friend of mine," Ana confirmed, "but a relatively *new* friend. I'd never heard him sound like that before. This boy was a 'good time,' always the life of the party, so when I heard his voice I *knew* he needed my help." A smile attempted to crack through the face mask. "It was so long ago! I should have just left it all behind me! That's what I intended to do when I left yesterday."

"It never hurts to confide in a new friend, does it?" Hans encouraged. "After all, it's not often I have conversations like this, with anyone. The men I deal with are all young and on the prowl, or stressed-out executives trying to pack three weeks of fun into a four-day weekend."

"Sounds like a night at The Tavern," Ana said, then explained, "This bar I used to go to in West Hollywood."

"I can imagine," Hans probed. "So this friend who called you on the phone? What did he need?"

"He needed my help." Ana got up to rinse off the mask. Hans led him to the bathroom, where he adjusted the temperature of the water. The thick face mask came off in large chunks.

Ana used a face wash to remove the remaining clay. Drying off his face with a thick bath towel, he smiled at what appeared to already be a younger, more relaxed man than the one who had awoken with a start, only hours earlier. "I thought maybe he was in jail. Or perhaps at an orgy gone awry. I mean, you never *knew* with this guy. But when he told me that he was in the hospital— that was when I began to be alarmed.

"It must have been maybe seven or eight in the morning, on a Sunday. I hadn't gone to bed until maybe four the night before. I'd had a big show on Sunset that night with a group of gender-bending pals. Well, when I got this call, I practically ran out of my apartment. Entering the hospital, I had no idea what to expect." Ana returned to the kitchen and sat back down.

"Looking back, I guess that was wise. Not knowing what to expect! What I saw, Hansito," he continued gravely, "was like nothing I could ever prepare myself for."

"What was your friend's name?"

"Chase Hastings. I don't know if you've heard the name or not," he said casually, as he stood up, taking it upon himself to make his own margarita. "At one point, he was a big adult film star."

"I...do...know the name...I think," Hans revealed carefully. "That must have been the same time I lived in L.A."

"Then you know how popular he was. We couldn't go anywhere without him being completely mobbed. But when I entered the hospital room that morning, *no one* was around. A nurse stood at the door, making sure I was Jen Bender. It turns out, I was the only one Chase had given authorization to come in to see him. I found *that* strange. We'd only *just* become friends, I couldn't figure out why he had singled *me* out. Well, there he was, in a full body cast, and what I *could* see of him was covered in cuts and bruises. His face was all puffed up with infection, his breathing was raspy."

"He'd been in a car accident!" Hans concluded, his own knowledge of the incident converging with Ana's confession.

"With two wannabe porn stars: the Barrington brothers. Mean and nasty bitches, both of them, and big-time users!" Ana said before clearing his throat. "May they rest in peace."

"So you mean you're the only one," Hans pondered, "who saw Chase Hastings before he died."

"Yes," Ana said reverently. "Chase did die that night."

He poured the tequila into the glass, giving it two quick stirs before sitting down. "But what no one else knows but me and a few select others who worked at the hospital that day, and now you, Hansito, is when Chase died, someone *else* was born! Chase was the only survivor of the accident, and the condition he was in at that point was critical. However, the moment he regained consciousness, he knew he had to do something quickly. He realized it the moment he felt that pain between his legs."

"I don't understand, Ana," Hans said, "What exactly are you saying?"

"Even though Chase Hastings had somehow managed to survive the accident, Hansito, a very important part of him had been, shall we say, severed."

Hans sat back. A chill went down his spine as he quickly crossed his legs. "Are you telling me that Chase Hastings lost his fabulous porn-star moneymaker in the accident?"

"You betta believe it. The Chase Hastings we all knew and jacked off to had, for all intents and purposes, died in the crash. It was up to me to help bring the new person lying there before me to a new life. To help shape that person into someone who could make something of his admittedly now-penis-less life."

Hans' jaw dropped open at the revelation, his eyes widening, as Ana revealed the details of Chase's dramatic transition.

"Initially," Ana continued, "we had a pile of hospital bills, and a doctor and nurse to pay off. Not to mention all the physical therapy. Eventually, however, he healed nicely, and we got my creation back to work and off to a brand-new start."

"How ever did you manage that?" Hans wondered.

"I put her to work on stage, of course!" Ana continued. "It was the only way to raise enough money to complete the boob job and facial reconstruction operations. But the closer she got to being completed, it seemed the more cunning and greedy she became. I don't know why! Maybe it was the hormones! If I could do it all over again, I would have left Chase Hastings there to die. All of him."

"And after everything you did to help him!" Hans was dumbfounded. "He would have been nothing without you!"

"Honey," Ana confessed with a dry laugh, "I even gave her the name she touts around today." Shrugging somewhat, he admitted, "Well…almost. At the time we were still raising money for her surgery, she went by the name of Anita Hoochie."

❖

It was almost four in the morning when the last of the night cleaners left The Tavern, shaking the gate to check that it was locked. Peering from binoculars half a block away, Jorge signaled that it was time to make a second attempt at entering Tucci's office.

Fumbling with the large set of keys, Beso tried each until he finally selected the correct one. Again, they made their way through the closed bar, dimly lit and silent. As they approached the stairs, Jorge heard a soft, shuffling sound from behind them.

"Did you hear that?" Jorge whispered to his cousin.

Beso shook his head and the two continued up the stairs. The shuffling sound continued, and then stopped as soon as they did. Making their way quickly up the steps, they heard the pace behind them increase. Bolting up the stairs, they could hear the sound closer behind.

"What's going on?" Beso asked as he ran to the door of Tucci's office.

"Just get in, and once we're inside, we'll lock it." Jorge, also nervous, looked back just as a man in black appeared from the shadows of the stairwell. A ski mask covered his face, allowing them only a glimpse of chestnut-colored eyes and pouty lips.

"I hope one of these keys will get us inside," Beso worried as he tried key after key to enter the frosted-glass door. Feeling a tap on his shoulder, he turned to see the man in black pointing a revolver at him and his cousin!

"Well, well," the assailant hissed, "if it isn't Cagney and Lacey, down Mexico way!"

"Good gravy!" Beso cried. "What do you want?"

With the gun still on the cousins, the intruder removed his ski mask with the other hand, rubbing his eyes and squinting as he looked at them.

"Phil Templeton!" Jorge gasped.

"We thought you were dead!" Beso said.

"Thanks for the flowers at my funeral, assholes!" he hissed. "I was the only one there!"

"I don't know if you noticed, Phil, but we're trying to help Nate Dainty on a manhunt," Jorge snapped. "So if you don't mind, just put away the revolver and go on your merry way."

"You heartless bitch! I should have hit you with the taco truck when I had the chance!"

"That was you?" Beso said.

"Well, if you're as good of a marksman as you are a driver, we have nothing to worry about," Jorge concluded.

"I'll leave you two alone," Phil agreed. "But first I want you to hand over the tape."

"No way!" Beso growled. "What do you want with this tape, anyway?"

"To bring Tucci, Needles, Bender, *everyone*, to their knees!" Phil barked. "Now hand it over."

"Okay, okay," Jorge agreed, taking the tape from Beso's book bag and slowly handing it over to Templeton. As Phil reached for the tape, Jorge raised his right leg in a quick kick, knocking the revolver from Phil's hand. Pushing him into the wall, Jorge grabbed the tape back and tossed it to his cousin.

"No!" Phil bellowed, coming back at Jorge.

Stooping down and rolling across the floor, Jorge tripped the assailant, who fell to the floor with a loud thud. Again, Phil leapt up, making another attempt at recovering the tape. With a hard strike to his torso and a firm blow with his knee, Jorge sent the attacker down a flight of stairs.

From above, they looked at the web designer, curled into

the fetal position and moaning. "Thank God I took that *pinche clase*." Jorge brushed himself off and walked back to the office door.

"Do you think he's all right?" Beso asked, alarmed.

"If he survived a blazing trailer, then a flight of stairs won't *kill* him. *Vámonos*, cousin!"

After trying several more keys, he ultimately slid a thick silver key in the slot and it turned with a click. In the office, the low hum of the audio-visual equipment brought an air of life into the room. Jorge's hands felt along the neatly organized desktop of the office until he found the switch to a small office light.

"Come on," Jorge whispered urgently. "Let's make this fast."

Beso knelt in front of the display of flat-screen monitors as he removed the large Betamax cassette from his book bag. He opened the glass cabinet beneath all the monitors, revealing an array of electronic panels. On the far right, a large silver machine purred loudly, the cover of the cassette feed reading *Betamax* in neon blue cursive.

"There!" He excitedly slipped the bright red plastic cassette in.

It took a few moments for the old machine to uncertainly whirr, digest the old tape and then slowly come back to life. Six televisions came on at once, and a shaky image appeared. The tape's tracking gradually self-adjusted, with low synthesized music punctuating the movements of a man's rear end as he strode down the street in tight yellow gym shorts and a tank top. The camera slowly panned the front of the man as he stopped in front of a gym. It took in his lithe swimmer's build and rose to reveal a boyishly handsome face, lightly covered in perspiration from his stroll. His blue eyes twinkled seductively as he pushed his loose curled blond hair off his forehead. His lips pursed as he breathed a long sigh.

Magic Afternoon, the title read, *starring Chase Hastings.*

"This is it! Beso! Look at him! He's a dead ringer for Myles Long," Jorge said in awe. "I wish Nate was here to see this for himself!"

Beso shook his head in disbelief. "He's a dead ringer for someone else, as well, but I can't quite place the face."

The film suddenly jumped to a clip of Chase Hastings playing tennis against a very accomplished competitor. Sweat glistened on his body. Hastings hit serve after serve until suddenly, after one serve, Hastings found the ball caught in the net. His opponent, a thinner, pimple-faced man with a lime green sweatband and brown hair, examined the ball with curiosity. Both looked on as the neon tennis ball remained stuck in the netting of the court. "Some serve," the pimply man said, amazed. "I've never seen that before. Must be a sign we need to call it a game." He shook Hastings' hand, and as he walked off, Chase heard the word "asshole" echo in his mind.

"Wait a minute," the hunk called out, voice smooth and sexy, "What did you call me?"

The guy looked back sheepishly, surprised by the question. "I didn't call you anything." He walked away, looking back once more at Chase. The star heard the same voice in his head. "At least, I didn't say that out loud. Or did I?"

"It's just as we thought, Beso," Jorge said. "So far *Magic Afternoon* is an *exact replica* of *The Straight Shooter*."

"Except Chase is playing tennis as opposed to Myles playing basketball. But yes," Beso agreed, "your suspicions are *correct*! Tucci would never want anyone to see this!"

"And, no one ever will!" a smooth, sexy voice a mere octave higher than the voice they had just heard on tape said from behind them.

The cousins turned to find themselves inches from a gleaming silver revolver. Beyond the pistol, they came face-to-face with Tucci herself, her expression twisted in outrage.

"Freeze, you little fuckers!" she commanded.

TOGETHER AT LAST

Something told me our paths would cross again," Myles said huskily as he stretched across the bed in a long yawn. Nate stood silent, catching quick glimpses of the tightly muscled body before him.

"Yes, although once again, not exactly what I had in mind," Nate said nervously, making out Long's soft smile in the moonlight.

Myles laughed tiredly and stood up, oblivious to the redhead's nudity. "Well," he said, gesturing to his accommodations, "it's a step up from the community college bathroom. Wow! You must have really been naughty! You didn't even get the regulation prison garb," he quipped, looking at his own gray jersey shorts and V-neck T-shirt.

"I guess I missed that during the check-in," Nate remarked dryly, still shocked at seeing the object of his manhunt right in front of him.

"What are you in for?" Myles asked with a wink. He leaned in and gave Nate a gentle kiss.

"Ironically enough, I put myself here. Looking for you."

"Now that you've found me, what next?" He looked at Nate searchingly. "Aside from the obvious, of course. I thought I was horny when I was free to roam the earth. Try being locked in a room for this long, right after meeting you."

He moved in to kiss the redhead, their lips locking softly as Myles teasingly slipped his tongue into Nate's mouth. Once again, Nate could feel the warmth of Long's body against his as their hands explored each other. With increasing determination, Myles pressed up against Nate, his breath heavy between the deep kisses. Hungrily, his hand slid down to Nate's backside, exploring where he'd left off—was it only a few days ago? Nate relaxed in his embrace, allowing Myles to stroke and then grip his erection, still sore from his earlier encounter.

"I'm sorry, Myles." Nate gently pushed Myles away. "I'm a bit worn out after being roughed up by your captor."

"So you've had the displeasure of meeting Mac Needles." Myles sat on the bed and motioned for Nate to join him.

"You could say that." Nate sat next to Myles, frustrated that their chance encounters continued to occur at the most inappropriate moments. "From the video I saw, I was sure that Needles was going to kill you."

"That's how he wanted it to look: the miracle of stage makeup," Myles agreed, referring to the mock snuff film. "I don't think he would have ever gone through with it. I will tell you one thing, though, the dude's absolutely obsessed with me. Seems like I look exactly like his old lover!"

"Chase Hastings," Nate said, "and that's why he abducted you."

"He had help from an old costar of mine, and soon-to-be former roommate, Buck Steers. But I guess Buck and Mac had some sort of disagreement over money or something 'cause since then it's just been me and Mac. I shouldn't complain. I'm just wondering when he's going to realize that I'm not this Chase character he wants me to be and give up."

"Somehow, I got that message through." Nate pulled the edge of a blanket across his lap. "But just as I thought he'd had this great psychological breakthrough, he tied me up and threw me into that 'secret room,' saying he had some unfinished business to take care of."

"That doesn't sound too good," Myles said gravely.

"What do *you* think it means? I mean, he kidnapped you because of your resemblance to Chase Hastings. Then what else could there be?"

"Apparently," Myles said as he ran his fingers over Nate's short red hair, "the movie I starred in—"

"The Straight Shooter?"

"The Straight Shooter. Despite its commercial success, and the obvious fanfare it's brought to me, it turns out that the concept of the movie wasn't so original after all. I suspect the revenge Needles is planning has to do with Anitra Tucci." He moved to the tall wardrobe and pushed open the upper cabinet to reveal a small television and video player.

"I found an old movie in this cabinet starring Mac Needles. I've only watched the beginning so far, but the resemblance to *The Straight Shooter* is uncanny."

"Do you mean to say Anitra Tucci stole the plot line?" Nate asked.

"Watch for yourself." Myles switched on the television and the movie began mid-scene, as Chase Hastings entered a mirrored office building lobby.

Pulling the door open, Hastings bumped into a secretary who was leaving. "Excuse me," he said courteously. The secretary, a svelte black drag queen with oversized shoulder pads, smiled and walked off. The word "jerk" echoed through Chase's mind. He shook his head, confused. "What a strange day I'm having," he said to himself.

"That voice sounds familiar," Nate said as the scene went on.

Chase Hastings walked through the lobby and rushed as he saw the elevator doors about to close. "Hold on," he called to the closing doors. He slid in just in the nick of time, and he came face-to-face with a businessman.

Nate hit the Pause button on a frame of the businessman. His face was line-free, a carefree and rugged sexiness glowed in his deep brown eyes: it was the 1986 version of their captor! As he pressed Play again, the camera zoomed in tight on Mac's warm, gentle gaze.

"I've been riding in the elevator with this guy three years now. What I'd give for the chance to have him." His voice— sweet and tinged with desire—echoed through Hastings' mind, then the two began to make out, slowly undoing one another's ties and shirt buttons as the camera circled them. Their kiss was long and passionate, the camera teasing the viewers as it revealed the next step of Hastings' calculated seduction.

Nate turned to Myles. "I guess *The Straight Shooter* wasn't such a ground-breaker after all."

"But did you notice the difference in the dialogue?" Myles said thoughtfully. "*The Straight Shooter* was just about fucking, but the scene with these two, they really make love!"

They watched again as Hastings and Needles, now fully undressed, made out in the elevator, their hands caressing each other, each kiss becoming deeper and more passionate. Mac rolled his head back, his eyes closed, as Chase slowly sank to the ground and took Needles' oversized tool in his mouth.

Nate bit his lip as he watched the scene, avoiding his attraction to the man he had found himself pursuing and, despite his sensibilities, craving more with each seductive glance, even in the frames of the worn tape. The murky shadows provided by the limited lighting in the scene made the passion between the two all the more tender.

"And to think hardly anyone remembers these two."

"That is a chilling thought," Myles agreed as the screen revealed Needles' massive cock slowly entering Chase. The camera swept rapidly up the star's taut swimmer's body to his face, revealing his pleasure.

"I mean, watching them on screen, I really get the passion between them," Nate said dreamily before turning around in surprise at his own reaction to the film. Despite his attempt to focus, his similar, far more recent encounter with Needles continued to replay in his memory.

"According to Mac, that's what destroyed him. I mean, look, he doesn't seem like a bad guy there, does he? When Chase Hastings died, it turned Mac desperate."

"What's this movie named?" Nate asked.

"*Magical Evening* or something like that."

"It's *Magic Afternoon*?" Nate jumped. "Don't you see? This is the movie Hastings never finished because of his fatal car accident."

"How do you know all this?"

"My houseboy was supposed to be in Scene Four," he admitted, and realizing Myles would have more questions, explained, "It's a long story. What's important is that without Chase Hastings, Needles was never able to finish this movie. In fact, *not finishing it* is what wrecked his life, as well as his career."

On screen, the couple enjoyed a final scene together—Needles bit Hastings' neck as he withdrew his cock and exploded against the blond's back. Pulling Chase closer to him, he again resumed their make-out session. Hastings also came, a slow-motion shot revealing each spasm.

"I don't understand," Myles said. "If the film wasn't finished, and if no one ever saw it, how could Anitra copy it after all these years?"

Almost as if in response to their question, the movie moved to its next scene, where Chase Hastings, satiated after his long elevator ride, sat at his desk and shuffled through papers. Examining the clock, he put his papers aside, and pressed the intercom buzzer.

"Mario? Has my sandwich arrived yet?" he questioned impatiently. On cue, the sandwich delivery guy entered, denim cut-offs revealing well-muscled, hairy legs, and a baseball jersey showing a healthy collection of gold chains.

"This is exactly like your scene with Gino Rantelli!" Nate exclaimed.

"Sorry I'm late," the swarthy Italian answered in the film as he set the sandwich on the desk.

"Do you plan on making it up to me?" the mind-reading businessman challenged. "You could at least offer me a free sandwich."

Obligingly, the delivery man nodded, but his thoughts echoed loud in Hastings' mind: "I'll give you more than a Turkey Club! I'll give you the blow job of your life!"

Smirking, Hastings then pressed the intercom button. "Mario! Bring me a bottle of Dom. And make it two glasses." Chase then unzipped his pants to reveal his own tool and popped it into the delivery man's waiting mouth.

As the camera panned up once again, Nate was startled to recognize the smile. "Rewind that scene!" Nate commanded, telling Myles to stop just as Hastings pressed the intercom a second time. As the scene played back, the soft and commanding tone of his words rang in Dainty's ears and transported him back to his first meeting in Tucci's office. He turned in amazement. "That's *it*! That's how Tucci knew about this movie's plot line."

"How?"

Grabbing the remote, Nate let the scene play until a tight close-up revealed Chase's knowing smirk. Hitting Pause, the redhead insisted, "Don't you see? Chase Hastings and Anitra Tucci are one and the same person!"

"Oh my God, I think you're right," the young porn star said.

"So, Mac Needles probably wants more than a showdown with Tucci. After how he's grieved, and after what he's gone through, he's probably ready to put this old lover business to rest—once and for all!"

"If that's true, we don't have much time to stop Mac before he does something he'll regret!"

They heard a creaking from the corridor leading to the secret room. As they clicked off the television, the room grew dark. Myles grabbed Nate's hand and they rushed into the corner of the room.

"Or maybe," Nate whispered, "he's already done it!" They heard the shuffling grow close. They could hear the clank of the metal panel as someone jumped into the room. In the darkness, they leapt upon the man as if on cue. Despite a brief struggle, the stranger, clad only in briefs, proved no match for the couple. Pushing their tightly muscled captor to the ground, they forced his hands behind his back. Nate now grabbed the ropes Needles had originally used to bind him.

Panting heavily, the man grew quiet as his arms and feet were bound. "Ay, *Papi*, this is more exciting than I ever imagined!" he moaned. Nate, finishing a tight knot, flipped their visibly aroused assailant over and gasped in shock. The faint glint of a silver tooth caught his eye.

"Manny Manos! It's like you and Needles are interchangeable."

"*Lo siento.* I missed you in the steam room," Manny said, a note of regret in his voice as he eyed first Nate, and then Myles, in recognition. He shifted to release the discomfort of his building erection. "But it looks like now I can have two *guapos* for the price of one."

"Not so fast, Manos!" Myles warned, putting an arm over his redheaded pal's shoulders. "How did you get in here?"

"Well," he wriggled on the floor, "I saw Mac as he was leaving the baths. He told me that now that he'd had a piece of your friend here, I could help myself to sloppy seconds!"

"Sloppy seconds?" Myles eyed Nate inquisitively.

"Well," Nate said, grateful the dim light covered his blush, "it was all in the interest of tracking you down. I didn't arrive here looking for a cheap fling—if that's what you're implying."

"You call our time in the shower *cheap*?" Manny asked in

a hurt tone. "*Papi,* that hot shower wasn't the only reason your man-pussy was wet!"

"Nate," Myles said, surprised.

"Listen here, you two-faced gigolo," Nate growled at Manos. "There's no way your sassy tales are going to keep me from being with the man I…like."

Myles looked at him admiringly, blue eyes beaming with appreciation.

"*Papi,*" Manos moaned, "I don't want to keep you from anything. I want *both* of you. Besides, Needles told me you were going to be tied up on a hook, buck-naked, waiting for action. All you have to do is untie these ropes, and I'll show you just how ready I am for you."

"Your *amigo* Needles," Nate revealed proudly, "obviously wasn't aware that I graduated from Gay Scouts with the highest honors. I can untie any knot any of you will ever make!"

"Sounds exciting," Myles said of the skills of his newfound suitor. "We'll have to try that knot business out sometime."

"Okay," Nate said, somewhat shaky from his escape, "but first we have actual work to do."

With Myles' help, he lifted Manos to his feet and dragged him through the small panel into the long corridor Nate had originally been in. The weight of Manos' body brushed against the couple, his erection still bulging through his tight briefs. A small sliver of light at the end of the hall revealed Manos had left the door from the steam room ajar.

"Ay, *Papis,*" Manos moaned, "take me now. This is the hottest scene I've ever been in."

"This isn't a 'scene,' you sex-crazed porn star," Nate scolded as he detected a second hook in the wall. Hooking Manny onto the prong, he said, "This is *real life.*"

"In that case," Manos retorted as he rubbed against the wall, "we need a good cameraman and better lighting, 'cause this is hella *caliente*!"

Both Nate and Myles eyed the man's bulging hard-on and then each other.

"You know, Nate," Myles said, cautiously. "I have to agree with my former costar on this one. It all is pretty hot."

"I must agree, as well. Neither of you are anything to sneeze at. However, first things first. We have to rescue Anitra!"

"What about me?" Manos wailed as the pair made their way out the ajar door. "You can't just leave me here all alone. I'm afraid of the dark!"

Nate turned one last time to the heavily muscled Latino, bound by the hook to the wall. "Don't worry, Manos," Nate promised with a sexy smile. "We'll both be back for you."

He slammed the door shut, again clicking the two benches of the steam room into an upright position. He quickly led Myles to the locker he'd put his clothes in earlier.

Myles gazed around the bathhouse, exhilarated. "Free at last!" he exclaimed. Turning to his friend with appreciation, he said, "And I owe it all to you!"

"We're not finished yet!" Nate reminded him as they raced, hand in hand, to his BMW. The car charged down Melrose and they each silently pondered Mac's next move.

A JARRING CONFESSION!

Well, well, Ms. Tucci," Jorge said evenly as he eyed the revolver, "allow *us* to explain."

"What on earth could there be that requires explanation?" Anitra sneered, as she backed away, her aim firm on the two cousins. "It's an everyday occurrence, finding two nosy snoops in my office, using my Betamax to watch unfinished eighties porn. No problem at all!"

"We're really sorry, Anitra," Beso said.

"Sorry doesn't begin to convey how you'll feel once I'm through with you." She glowered, teeth clenched, her face taut. "You have no idea how your nosiness has messed up my life! But," she walked to her desk, "since you want to know everything, then you will."

One hand steadied the gun aimed at the two; with the other she reached for a remote on the desk and paused the on-screen scene. Chase Hastings' face froze. "How did you two *get* this movie?"

Tears welling, Beso looked helplessly at Jorge. Jorge's lip began to quiver in fear.

"Tell me how you got hold of this tape!" Tucci demanded.

"From Ana Bender," Beso confessed, his voice beginning to shake as he wept. "Please, Anitra! We didn't mean any harm."

"The hell you didn't! That fucking Ana Bender!" Anitra

wailed. "Wasn't half a million enough for that bitch?" She made her way to the bar and lifted a bottle of champagne out of the cooler. "I never should have called her that day. Never! Would you like a glass?" Her voice returned to its usual purr.

"No—thanks," Beso said.

"Boys! I insist!" She filled three glasses. "I've saved this bottle especially for a night like tonight." With her gun fixed on the boys, she handed each a glass, then raised up her own flute. "A toast," she said snidely, "to shocking revelations!"

Beso and Jorge's hands shook as they toasted.

"Drink it!" she snapped. "Don't make me feel like I'm wasting money."

"We didn't know," Jorge insisted, "what we got ourselves into."

"Really, Anitra," Beso agreed, "we had no idea *Magic Afternoon* was so similar to *The Straight Shooter*. Coming on it was a complete coincidence."

"We're prepared to say *absolutely nothing*," Jorge said urgently. "So how about we finish our champagne and call it a night?"

Anitra laughed softly. "Fat chance," she bellowed, looking at Beso's gut. "Look at the young man on the screen. He had *so much* going for him. Everything was just coming into place."

"Until his car accident," Beso said. "We know the whole story, Anitra."

Her eyebrows raised in surprise at the statement. "The whole story?" she challenged. "*No one* knows the *whole story*. Not even that swollen, beat-up old gender-bending drunk." She took a long gulp of champagne and set it down. Resting on the edge of the desk, she looked over at the two. "No one knows the whole story—that is, except me."

"We heard this movie was going to change the way men watched porn," Jorge said softly, with hope. "That the attraction Hastings and Needles shared on screen and off was similar to that of Hollywood Legends."

"It would have changed *everything*!" Tucci agreed, and her hand relaxed its hold on the pistol. "And, eventually, it did. Only the roles now are played by younger men, men who were barely able to walk when the original was filmed. But what I *can* tell you, boys, is that all these years I have been trying to get that time back."

"Were you involved in the production of *Magic Afternoon*, too?" Beso asked, amazed. "I had no idea your career spanned that far."

"Don't let my youthful appearance fool you." Anitra pressed Play on the Betamax as the scene between Needles and Hastings resumed. "It may surprise you to know I have a very special keepsake originating from the time *Magic Afternoon* was produced."

"Really?" Beso asked with naïve interest as he watched the screens.

Needles held Hastings around the waist with one arm, the other over his shoulder as he made love to the attractive blond. The camera moved tight on Hastings; one of Mac's hands steadied him against the elevator while the other rapidly beat off his large member.

Tucci refilled her champagne and paused the frame.

"Such a beautiful scene," she said, a tear glistening. "It would have made history!" She pulled at a silver chain around her neck that revealed a small key and removed the necklace before making her way to a filing cabinet. "And now," she said with sadness, "all that's left of that scene is right here." Producing a leather-bound case, she presented it to the cousins. "Go ahead! Jorge! Open it!"

Trembling, Jorge's hand unlatched the leather case, revealing a large object wrapped in crushed blue velvet. "What is it?" Jorge asked with grave uncertainty.

"Allow me to help," Tucci offered. She grabbed the object, propping it upon the desktop, still sheathed in heavy blue fabric. She lifted the fabric off with a snap.

"What is it?" Beso wailed fearfully, his eyes shut tightly.

"A bundle of love letters," Tucci said simply. Untying the bundle, she threw the letters at the cousins. Relaxing, Beso grabbed one of the envelopes and pulled out a yellowed piece of stationery.

"Dear Mac," Beso read, before flipping to the last page of the letter. "These are all written by Chase Hastings?"

"Yes, each and every one of them. On the date of their anniversary. No matter how you try, some pieces of the past just can't be erased."

"Wait a minute," Beso said, "The date on this letter is June 26, 2003. Chase Hastings died in 1986."

"He did. Part of him died in that car wreck. Unfortunately, the one part that survived is the hardest part to satisfy."

"His heart," Beso finished, moved despite the circumstances. "But how did you—"

Tucci stood silently, nodding to the monitor that held the image of her former self.

"Do you mean to tell us—*you're Chase Hastings*?" Jorge asked.

"Not anymore. I was," she removed her emerald green contacts, revealing Chase's unforgettable trademark blue eyes, "but not anymore."

"You've kept this secret all these years?" Beso marveled.

"And I'll continue to. Once I finish your meddlesome asses off." She raised the revolver in defiance.

"But why?"

"Without that marvelous cock, Chase Hastings was as good as dead. After the accident, my penis couldn't be found, the police decided it probably burned inside the car, along with the Barrington twins—those dreadful sluts."

"So how did Ana get involved?" Jorge questioned.

"I didn't want to face the world without what had made me famous. I couldn't. I called Ana and asked for help to give me a new life."

"Ana helped you in your transformation?" Beso said.

"'Help' is a questionable term," Tucci said bitterly. "We'd agreed to keep it all a secret. I bribed the officiating doctors to pronounce Chase Hastings dead. I'd requested cremation without any body viewing in my will. Not even Mac saw it." Her voice trailed off sadly.

"So why was it questionable? If Ana cooperated with your requests?" Jorge asked.

"Oh trust me, I've heard every day, all these years, how lucky I am that Bender saved me. How much I owed him for making me what I am today. And no matter how hard I tried, Mac would never accept me for who I'd become as a result of the accident."

"That is so cruel!" Beso declared. "Here you've been supporting Bender all this time and this is what he does to you?"

"Nothing was ever enough," Tucci said. "When my aunt Frannie passed away, I gave him the condo I inherited just to buy his silence, but that only made him want more. I had to keep building this empire to keep that old queen's mouth shut. For years, I had thought about releasing *The Straight Shooter*. The movie lived on in my mind since the accident. But I didn't want to do it until I could assemble the perfect cast. Meeting Myles Long was the catalyst to completing the film."

"And it's your biggest hit yet!" Jorge reminded her comfortingly. "You must be proud!"

She sighed and released her hold on the revolver, setting it on the desk. "I wanted to be," Tucci agreed, "but even that didn't go unscathed. Bender told me then that he still held what he believed to be the final copy of *Magic Afternoon*. He knew revealing the unfinished film could destroy me."

"In more ways than one," Beso said.

"I couldn't take the stress of keeping all my secrets any longer. The phone calls from Bender, along with Myles Long's abduction, were about to send me over the edge. I finally told Bender to name his price. I'd do whatever it took to get him out of my life, once and for all."

"And it worked," Jorge said.

"Except," Tucci added, "he failed to deliver on one part of the deal."

"Which was?" Beso questioned.

"To return Myles Long. That's why I agreed in the first place, because I wanted my headliner back."

The cousins looked at each other. "I think we have more bad news for you, Anitra," Beso said. "You were totally hoodwinked on that."

"What do you mean?"

"Bender never *had* Myles Long in his possession," Jorge said.

"Then who did?" Tucci asked.

"I did." The voice came from the hall. A figure emerged in the office door, clad in tight jeans, a black leather coat, and a look of intense sadness. Mac Needles!

"I have Myles, Chase." He stepped into the room.

"How long have you been out there?" Tucci asked.

"Long enough," he gently touched Tucci, "to know what kept us apart all these years. And to finally understand why you did what you did."

"I never wanted to hurt you, Mac. As crazy as this must sound, I did this all to protect you. Bender told me I'd only cause you pain."

"The only pain you caused me in my life was when you weren't in it," Mac said softly. "I was determined to get even with this monster, Anitra Tucci, this big-time producer who had brought all my memories back from the dead. It wasn't until the night I came here to rattle her cage a bit that I realized she was really you."

"That was you?" Anitra said, surprised. "I thought it was some thug Ana had hired."

"It was when you turned your neck, and I saw that mole behind your ear, that I realized. All these years, and now you've come back to me."

"But not entirely," Tucci said. "I can never be the same."

"Really, only one thing remains unchanged. That I still love you."

"How sweet!" Beso gushed.

"I didn't understand…" Mac confessed. "But seeing our movie again, I saw the similarity between you and Myles Long. That was all it took to make me snap back. I had finally gotten my life in order, after years of darkness. But seeing someone on screen who looked like you way back then—it was too much for me to take."

"I wanted to finish it—once and for all," Tucci said. "To have part of *you* back, too!"

"If you want, you can have *all* of me."

The two kissed, and Beso grabbed a fourth champagne flute off the bar.

"Well," Jorge exclaimed, "this definitely calls for a toast."

Just then, the frosted-glass door swung open with a crash. Nate and Myles Long leapt into the room with drawn guns.

"Freeze, fuckers!" Nate cried.

The four, glasses aloft in a toast, looked at them and then laughed. Beso quickly went to the bar for two more flutes.

"Nate Dainty," Anitra Tucci laughed as she dried her eyes with a tissue, "stop stealing my best lines!"

ESTRANGED BEDFELLOWS

"Nathan! Wake up," Hans called, lightly tapping the redhead's bedroom door late the following afternoon. "I have a delicious breakfast made for you and your new friend."

"Be right there, Hans," Nate mumbled sleepily as he rolled over in his bed into Myles Long's arms. The sun peeked through plantation shutters, coating the couple in a warm, orange glow.

"Is it time to wake up?" Long asked as he kissed Nate's forehead. The two explored each other's bodies through the soft, down-filled blankets, and Nate groggily kissed Long. "Part of me's been awake for you all week!"

Making out, the two caved in to each other's passions, easily done now that they were well rested after the all-night escapade that had reunited not one, but two couples. Slowly, Myles pried his lips away from Nate's, sliding down along his neck and trailing to his chest, his tongue circling each nipple before taking it into his mouth, sucking greedily as Nate moaned. Closing his eyes, Nate grabbed hold of the curled head that was pleasuring him and pushed it down lower, feeling his hardening cock slide into Myles' warm mouth.

Myles let out a soft moan and took the cock deep, his arm sliding beneath Nate's backside, raising him up. Savoring each lick, Nate moaned as Myles backed away, gave him a soft gaze, and then used both hands to lift Nate's ankles into the air, the porn star's stubble tickling Nate's legs as Myles tongued his hole. Resisting the urge to moan loudly, Nate bit his lip, turning his head to the side as he felt himself loosening to Myles' advances.

Keeping Nate's legs in the air, Myles kissed along the inside of his thighs as he moved back to eye level. "Ready?" he asked with a sleepy smile.

"Finally. Yes!" Nate said. Toying with Nate, Long allowed the head of his cock to enter Nate as the pair made out, their mouths damp with desire. Entering him, Long pressed his lips tight to Nate's, silencing them as their bodies rubbed together.

"Nathan Dainty! I am *not* kidding!" Hans yelled from the other side of the door. "Your eggs are getting cold."

"Coming!" Nate cried as they writhed. Myles' blue eyes flashed appreciatively at Nate as they quickly prepared for breakfast.

"I can definitely get used to this," Myles grabbed a towel off Nate before giving him a quick peck on the cheek.

"So could I," Nate agreed, but his mind kept going back to another encounter, far more breathtaking in Nate's opinion, from not so long ago. At last, they emerged at the breakfast nook. Pancakes, scrambled eggs, fresh fruit and juices all lay spread on the kitchen island, as Hans continued to cook.

"Wake up, sleepyheads."

"Yes, I am simply starving," Beso quipped, coming out from around the corner. At the kitchen table was seated not only Jorge, but also Mac Needles and Anitra Tucci!

"Celebrating your success, Nate Dainty. Without you, none of this could have happened!" She held her glass of champagne up in greeting.

"Well," Nate said uncomfortably, briefly locking eyes with Needles. "It was a lengthier process than I thought it would be!"

"Well worth it, I hope?" Needles questioned, his smile sexy and knowing.

"Oh! Very!" Nate's face reddened. Finding a place next to Myles, he began to eat and they all dug into the breakfast.

"What time is it?" Myles asked.

"Almost five p.m.," Jorge said. "Nate Dainty! This manhunt of yours has really screwed up my sleeping schedule."

"All I can say is thank heavens it's over," Hans declared, "because Hansito's Hideaway was one very hard-to-manage resort!"

"Too many difficult guests?" Beso chided between bites of pancake.

"One in particular," Hans wailed.

"Well, you'll all be pleased to know that your guest, Ms. Ana Bender, is safely ensconced in a rehab facility somewhere in Central Iowa," Tucci revealed. "The world has given me a second chance. So I only thought it suitable to give the one who started it all the same opportunity."

"Very admirable of you, Anitra." Nate beamed. "I'm sure Ana will have a good time with all those corn-fed Iowa boys!"

The table laughed again until Hans got up. "Oh no you don't! Nate Dainty! Don't even *think* about going off on another manhunt."

"Don't worry, Hans," Myles put an arm around Nate, "I won't let him."

"At least not until our new film is completed," Tucci said firmly. "When Mac went to release Manny Manos from the secret room at Vapor Baths, he came up with a brilliant idea for a new movie. It just screams 'hit.'"

"And," Needles eyed Nate again, "he wants Myles and Nate as his costars."

The couple looked at each other for permission before nodding eagerly.

"It's a date!" Nate said enthusiastically.

"Ay caramba!" Jorge said, "Save some men for the rest of us, Nate Dainty!"

Nate smiled at all the attention and relaxed in the arms of his long-lost suitor. "Don't worry, Jorge, I can think of no place I'd rather be than here with my good friends."

"Here, here!" Beso agreed as he stood up. "To Nate Dainty!"

"To Nate Dainty," they cheered.

"And," Tucci also stood and rested a hand on Mac's shoulder, "to magical afternoons like this."

The glasses clinked musically as the autumn sun surrendered to night. While they enjoyed the late breakfast, the sound of cheering and chanting voices came from beyond the gated entrance.

Getting up in alarm, Hans rushed to the door, opened it, and was shocked to find a sea of people in front of the Dainty home.

"He's found!" the crowd, a bevy of gay men wearing Tucci's trademark "Find Him!" tank top, enthusiastically cheered. "He's found!"

Hans walked out into the swarm and the cheers switched to a low boo. "We want Myles!" they demanded. "Bring out Myles!"

Hans shrugged and went back into the house. "Something tells me I'm not gonna cut it," he said. The phone rang as the houseboy reentered, and his eyes brightened at the display of the caller ID. "It's your uncle Carter! Just wait until I tell him what you've all been up to!" The houseboy clicked his tongue as he answered the phone, escaping into the privacy of the den.

Anitra looked at her young star with delight. "We certainly can't keep your fans waiting! Can we?" she asked, motioning for Long to make his way out to the crowd.

Beso and Jorge followed, along with Needles, and Tucci close behind. Upon seeing Myles Long, the crowd roared deafeningly. Nate covered his ears with his hands, pushed the door shut, and sat back down at the table.

At that moment, Nate felt how Myles Long must have felt in the ending of *The Straight Shooter*:

A late session on the basketball court had finally dislodged the stuck ball from the net. It landed with a heavy thud on the gym's hardwood. Suddenly, Long's mind-reading abilities disappeared and his brain became void of the secret thoughts that had filled his day. The hot pursuits, filled with the music of other people's desires and passions, suddenly screeched to a stop like a needle being ripped off an unforgettable record. The camera closing in, Myles sat alone in his bedroom. Once again, he had sadly become just an ordinary man. "What happened?" Myles asked in the final scene, just before the credits rolled.

Alone in the breakfast nook, Nate found himself asking the same question.

Anitra whirled back into the room, closed the door behind her, her blue eyes wild with excitement. Then she noticed Nate alone at the table. "Unbelievable!" she exclaimed. "The fanfare for Myles!"

"Beyond anything you could ever imagine?" Nate asked, watching her as she grabbed a compact to examine herself. Correcting a scarcely noticeable flaw in her makeup, she kept her gaze firmly on her reflection as she spoke.

"It certainly is! I don't think *I* could have created such a buzz if I'd started it myself," she marveled, closing the compact.

"You should give yourself more credit," Nate replied, standing up to face the producer. "After all, if it weren't for your release of *The Straight Shooter*, none of this would have happened."

She turned and slowly lowered the compact, her face darkening at his statement before she forced out a defiant laugh. "What on earth are you implying, Nate Dainty?"

"Isn't this, exactly," Nate continued, knowingly, "how you thought things would turn out all along? Tucci Productions needed a financial jolt after all of its acquisitions, and *The Straight Shooter* gave it just the fix it needed."

"Darling, that's no secret! Even you were enamored of the movie all summer long," she countered.

"It's still my favorite. For obvious reasons, I prefer it over the *original*," Nate said, eyeing the former star with measurable distaste. "But you had to do *more* than just make a great film, Anitra!

"You had to do something to provide you with an unthinkably huge amount of publicity. To make enough money so that you could thwart Ana Bender's threats and still come out looking like the good gal in the situation."

"You think I wanted Mac to abduct Myles? Have you lost your community college–educated mind?" She turned to the doorway and pulled it ajar. The sound of the crowd once again rose above their conversation.

Nate held the door before Tucci could make an exit.

"There's no other way this could have worked out. You knew the effect this movie would have on Mac. I believe you also knew the response that it would trigger not only from him, but the press, too! No wonder you asked me not to report Myles' abduction right away. It gave you all the time you needed to assemble all those Myles Long tank tops!"

Tucci turned to Nate, a brief helpless moment against his tide of accusations.

"Anitra." Mac rushed up to her, pushing the door out of Nate's grip. "Channel Five is here! They want to interview you and Myles for the Eleven O'Clock News!"

She gazed at Nate another moment, regained her composure, and purred, "Thank you, Mac." She slowly turned her head to the crowd and made her way down into the flashing press cameras, cheers growing louder as she appeared.

Nate walked away and headed to the French doors at the back of the house, his mind racing.

"I've never seen anything like this," Mac said with a soft laugh, making his way to the young redhead. "I must say! Our respective partners certainly have a way with the media."

"I have to agree." Nate covered his disappointment as he turned to Mac.

"Maybe more than you bargained for," Mac rested his hand

on Nate's shoulder. "I mean, here you finally have Myles Long all to yourself, and the real world swoops in and takes him away from you."

"The same could be said for you." Nate's mood was still clouded by the crowd. "Now that reality is setting in, will Anitra Tucci be able to satisfy all those unquenched memories of Chase Hastings?"

Mac froze, locking eyes with Nate. Nate turned to look out the French doors. "I don't honestly know if that'll happen," Mac admitted. He stepped beside Nate, sharing his view of the back yard, his hand still resting over the redhead's shoulder.

"But I *can* tell you the empty feeling I had all those years is slowly going away. In fact," he continued, turning Dainty around and grabbing him by his side, "I feel better than I've felt in a long time."

"I know," Nate said cautiously. "It's the same for me."

"It's good to be wanted, isn't it?" Mac said, looking deep into Nate's eyes.

"Yes," Nate said to the man he'd spent so much time searching for, "as long as you're wanted by the right guy."

"Are you wanted by the right guy?" The heat of Mac's breath caused Nate's face to flush.

"I don't know. Am I?" Nate asked as stillness returned to the room. A question so basic and straightforward was now suddenly laced with complications.

"That should be obvious."

The door swung open once again, and the two parted and turned to Beso excitedly coming into the room.

"Come on guys, they want shots of *all of us* for the morning papers!" He motioned them out before rushing back out into the crowd. Hand in hand, they turned to the doorway and made their way out to the crowd of Myles Long's most devoted fans.

❖

"Well the good news, Carter, is that Nathan and his friends are now out of harm's way," Hans said over the phone as he strolled back into the breakfast nook. He exchanged good-byes with Nate's concerned uncle and carefully set the receiver onto the table.

"Just as I was beginning to enjoy all this action," Hans murmured sadly before the vacant breakfast table. The used dishes provided the only reminder of the group's recent adventures. "I guess Nathan's—and my own—manhunt days are officially over."

Little did the aging houseboy or any of them know, however, that another mystery would soon develop, and Nate and the cousins would find themselves in a sea of troubles, cruising the Mexican Riviera aboard *The Vicious Queen*.

About the Author

Paul Faraday was raised on an unbalanced diet of prime-time soaps, unrequited high school crushes, and 80s power ballads in northern Minnesota. He lives in Las Vegas with his partner and is octomom to a group of unruly houseplants. *The Straight Shooter* is his first novel.

Books Available From Bold Strokes Books

Chasing Love by Ronica Black. Amy Edwards is looking for love—at girl bars, shady chat rooms, and women's sporting events—but love remains elusive until she looks closer to home. (978-1-60282-192-7)

Rum Spring by Yolanda Wallace. Rebecca Lapp is a devout follower of her Amish faith and a firm believer in the Ordnung, the set of rules that govern her life in the tiny Pennsylvania town she calls home. When she falls in love with a young "English" woman, however, the rules go out the window. (978-1-60282-193-4)

Indelible by Jove Belle. A single mother committed to shielding her child from the parade of transient relationships she endured as child tries to resist the allure of a tattoo artist who already has a sometimes-girlfriend. (978-1-60282-194-1)

The Straight Shooter by Paul Faraday. With the help of his good pals Beso Tangelo and Jorge Ramirez, Nate Dainty tackles the Case of the Missing Porn Star, none other than his latest heartthrob—Myles Long! (978-1-60282-195-8)

Head Trip by D.L. Line. Shelby Hutchinson, a young computer professional, can't wait to take a virtual trip. She soon learns that chasing spies through Cold War Europe might be a great adventure, but nothing is ever as easy as it seems—especially love. (978-1-60282-187-3)

Desire by Starlight by Radclyffe. The only thing that might possibly save romance author Jenna Hardy from dying of boredom during a summer of forced R&R is a dalliance with Gardner Davis, the local vet—even if Gard is as unimpressed with Jenna's charms as she appears to be with Jenna's fame. (978-1-60282-188-0)

River Walker by Cate Culpepper. Grady Wrenn, a cultural anthropologist, and Elena Montalvo, a spiritual healer, must find a way to end the River Walker's murderous vendetta—and overcome a maze of cultural barriers to find each other. (978-1-60282-189-7)

Blood Sacraments, edited by Todd Gregory. In these tales of the gay vampire, some of today's top erotic writers explore the duality of blood lust coupled with passion and sensuality. (978-1-60282-190-3)

Mesmerized by David-Matthew Barnes. Through her close friendship with Brodie and Lance, Serena Albright learns about the many forms of love and finds comfort for the grief and guilt she feels over the brutal death of her older brother, the victim of a hate crime. (978-1-60282-191-0)

Whatever Gods May Be by Sophia Kell Hagin. Army sniper Jamie Gwynmorgan expects to fight hard for her country and her future. What she never expects is to find love. (978-1-60282-183-5)

nevermore by Nell Stark and Trinity Tam. In this sequel to *everafter*, Vampire Valentine Darrow and Were Alexa Newland confront a mysterious disease that ravages the shifter population of New York City. (978-1-60282-184-2)

Playing the Player by Lea Santos. Grace Obregon is beautiful, vulnerable, and exactly the kind of woman Madeira Pacias usually avoids, but when Madeira rescues Grace from a traffic accident, escape is impossible. (978-1-60282-185-9)

Midnight Whispers: The Blake Danzig Chronicles by Curtis Christopher Comer. Paranormal investigator Blake Danzig, star of the syndicated show *Haunted California* and owner of Danzig Paranormal Investigations, has been able to see and talk to the dead since he was a small boy, but when he gets too close to a psychotic spirit, all hell breaks loose. (978-1-60282-186-6)

The Long Way Home by Rachel Spangler. They say you can't go home again, but Raine St. James doesn't know why anyone would want to. When she is forced to accept a job in the town she's been publicly bashing for the last decade, she has to face down old hurts and the woman she left behind. (978-1-60282-178-1)

Water Mark by J.M. Redmann. PI Micky Knight's professional and personal lives are torn asunder by Katrina and its aftermath. She needs to solve a murder and recapture the woman she lost—while struggling to simply survive in a world gone mad. (978-1-60282-179-8)

Picture Imperfect by Lea Santos. Young love doesn't always stand the test of time, but Deanne is determined to get her marriage to childhood sweetheart Paloma back on the road to happily ever after, by way of Memory Lane—and Lover's Lane. (978-1-60282-180-4)

The Perfect Family by Kathryn Shay. A mother and her gay son stand hand in hand as the storms of change engulf their perfect family and the life they knew. (978-1-60282-181-1)

Raven Mask by Winter Pennington. Preternatural Private Investigator (and closeted werewolf) Kassandra Lyall needs to solve a murder and protect her Vampire lover Lenorre, Countess Vampire of Oklahoma—all while fending off the advances of the local werewolf alpha female. (978-1-60282-182-8)

The Devil be Damned by Ali Vali. The fourth book in the best-selling Cain Casey Devil series. (978-1-60282-159-0)

Descent by Julie Cannon. Shannon Roberts and Caroline Davis compete in the world of world-class bike racing and pretend that the fire between them is just professional rivalry, not desire. (978-1-60282-160-6)

Kiss of Noir by Clara Nipper. Nora Delaney is a hard-living, sweet-talking woman who can't say no to a beautiful babe or a friend in danger—a darkly humorous homage to a bygone era of tough broads and murder in steamy New Orleans. (978-1-60282-161-3)

Under Her Skin by Lea Santos Supermodel Lilly Lujan hasn't a care in the world, except life is lonely in the spotlight—until Mexican gardener Torien Pacias sees through Lilly's facade and offers gentle understanding and friendship when Lilly most needs it. (978-1-60282-162-0)

Fierce Overture by Gun Brooke. Helena Forsythe is a hard-hitting CEO who gets what she wants by taking no prisoners when negotiating—until she meets a woman who convinces her that charm may be the way to win a battle, and a heart. (978-1-60282-156-9)

Trauma Alert by Radclyffe. Dr. Ali Torveau has no trouble saying no to romance until the day firefighter Beau Cross shows up in her ER and sets her carefully ordered world aflame. (978-1-60282-157-6)

Wolfsbane Winter by Jane Fletcher. Iron Wolf mercenary Deryn faces down demon magic and otherworldly foes with a smile, but she's defenseless when healer Alana wages war on her heart. (978-1-60282-158-3)

Little White Lie by Lea Santos. Emie Jaramillo knows relationships are for other people, and beautiful women like Gia Mendez don't belong anywhere near her boring world of academia—until Gia sets out to convince Emie she has not only brains, but beauty…and that she's the only woman Gia wants in her life. (978-1-60282-163-7)

Witch Wolf by Winter Pennington. In a world where vampires have charmed their way into modern society, where werewolves walk the streets with their beasts disguised by human skin, Investigator Kassandra Lyall has a secret of her own to protect. She's one of them. (978-1-60282-177-4)

Do Not Disturb by Carsen Taite. Ainsley Faraday, a high-powered executive, and rock music celebrity Greer Davis couldn't be less well suited for one another, and yet they soon discover passion has a way of designing its own future. (978-1-60282-153-8)

From This Moment On by PJ Trebelhorn. Devon Conway and Katherine Hunter both lost love and neither believes they will ever find it again—until the moment they meet and everything changes. (978-1-60282-154-5)

Vapor by Larkin Rose. When erotic romance writer Ashley Vaughn decides to take her research into the bedroom for a night of passion with Victoria Hadley, she discovers that fact is hotter than fiction. (978-1-60282-155-2)

Wind and Bones by Kristin Marra. Jill O'Hara, award-winning journalist, just wants to settle her deceased father's affairs and leave Prairie View, Montana, far, far behind—but an old girlfriend, a sexy sheriff, and a dangerous secret keep her down on the ranch. (978-1-60282-150-7)

Vieux Carré Voodoo by Greg Herren. Popular New Orleans detective Scotty Bradley just can't stay out of trouble—especially when an old flame turns up asking for help. (978-1-60282-152-1)